AF436835

Settlers

A Western Novel

Richard G. Hole

Far West

SYNOPSIS

It is not surprising that the History of Humanity, and in this case of North America, is full of heroic or bloody episodes for the possession of the land.

The audacious pioneers who opened the routes of the American West fought and died to conquer it for their benefit.

They fought to the death against the wild Indians for taking from them hundreds of hectares that the Reds did not cultivate, but did hold to protect the game that was their main food.

Later, when the victors in this tragic struggle managed to settle down and get the property, sometimes conquered with blood and with sensitive losses between both sides ...

Settlers is a story belonging to the Far West collection, a collection of novels developed in the American Wild West.

SETTLERS

CHAPTER I

SO ABILENE WAS BORN

The earth is the mother of humanity because she is the one that provides the rational and irrational with the basis of their livelihood, but she is a common mother for all, although it happens that some of her children, more selfish and ambitious than others, do. they want all of her, even at the cost of the sacred part that corresponds to their brothers.

So it is not surprising that the History of Humanity, and in this case of North America, is full of heroic or bloody episodes for the possession of the land.

The audacious pioneers who opened the routes of the American West fought and died to conquer it for their benefit.

They fought to the death against the wild Indians for taking from them hundreds of hectares that the Reds did not cultivate, but did hold to protect the game that was their main food.

Later, when they were victorious in this tragic struggle, they managed to settle down and get the property, sometimes conquered with blood and with sensitive losses between both sides, the ambitious, the selfish, the strong came behind, for grouping themselves into gangs, and disputed them. those fertile lands, for whose achievement they had exposed nothing to conquer them.

These were the spurious children of mother earth, those who wanted everything and tried to take it away from those who had gotten the right thing, and this caused that throughout the plains and prairies, where the virgin soil was offered to the bold that traveled thousands of miles to take possession of them, innumerable pages of blood were written, because the one who had risked his life to conquer those lands, did not agree to others, no matter how bold and powerful, would try to take them away.

One of the most fertile states in land, especially as a result of the Civil War, which was, when the North seized them, holding them almost exclusively for thirty years, was Kansas. This state, divided into three platforms of different heights, offered especially in its eastern part everything that the farmer and rancher could wish for their ears or their cattle. It was the most fertile of all, since the western plain was almost arid, drab with very few trees, cut by the valleys of the Arkansas and the Smoky Hille River, in which many fossils and caravan remains were found, crushed by the storms of ice and sand during the daring marches of the aforementioned routes.

This territory was known only to the Oregon, Osages and Black Dogs Indians, until the year 1541, when the famous Spanish explorer Coronado, accompanied by his troops, arrived in search of gold to a place that is believed to have been between the cities. of Great Bend and Junción City, current names of these towns.

At that time, according to the chronicles of some audacious travelers who traveled part of the territory, it was known for "the belt of blue grasses" and its soil offered four kinds of invaluable grass: The so-called "turkey foot", "bearded grass "," Green thistle "and" the grass of love ", classes that still exist, very cared for by farmers.

But against these excellencies of the land, it was necessary to count on its terrible sandstorms that dragged the mulch in an area of nine million in one breath over the roofs of the granaries and killed the cattle, dragging them like feathers.

But no farmer or rancher could settle down with peace of mind until the war was over and the "Union Pacific" was inaugurated. This peace was achieved through the non-aggression treaty with the Indians and it was from this date that the colonization of what has come to be called "the granary of America" really began.

It was shortly before the outbreak of the Civil War, when a compact group of "desperate" gathered in a caravan, set out in the footsteps of the Santa Fe route, seeking territorial expansion for their desire to live. Overcrowded states offered few possibilities, and the land in such places was more than spread out and exploited.

Only by leaving civilization behind and looking for horizons that were not explored if not exploited, could it be obtained plots of land without an owner to claim them or to demand royalties that their poverty could not pay.

You had to expose a lot to get something and they did not hesitate to expose it.

Leaving the eastern part of the country behind them, already almost filled, they entered the heart of the State, and thus, one day, they arrived at a place where forces and resources seemed to have reached their peak.

This place was nestled in the western part and later, someone baptized it with the strange name of Abilene.

It was true that this was not the most ideal part of Kansas, but it had an advantage: the chosen place was along the riverbed of Smoky Hill and the benefit of the water made all the land that extended along its banks, It was as uddly and promising as they were looking for it.

The caravan consisted of about eighty men, women and children and was led by an energetic old man, who had previously been a caravanner and who was partly familiar with the routes and the terrain.

All the settlers came from the East and had had to make a difficult journey of hundreds of miles, until they dug their heels into that piece of the State. Exhausted, haggard, some with only skin sticking to their bones, they flopped down into the thick grass and vowed not to have the courage to go on any further.

Either they settled there through thick and thin, facing the new hardships that would be presented to them to found and maintain the town, or they would allow themselves to die facing the sun or swept away by a sandstorm.

The most prominent of the caravan met in consultation, the pros and cons were studied and it was decided by majority of opinions to settle there.

The place had an advantage: the river, with its beneficial influence on its crops, but without communication routes. The railroad that three or four years later was to cross the State on its way to the coast, would pass through about twenty miles, were insignificant for the life of a town and could well withstand its arrival. It would be the time that they calculated necessary for their properties to yield to the maximum and then it could be taking advantage of the railroad to send their products to the East and West.

And there they stayed in community, not without first noticing the old guide named Víctor Bird:

"Comrades, it is not hidden from us that we are going to go through some tremendous months of deprivation and anguish until our future crops give enough to feed us and I say nothing until we can make a profit from them. This can be possible if we sacrifice ourselves in favor of others, according to the possibilities of each one.

"In this caravan we have gathered men and women from different states; Some better endowed than others, arrive with provisions and items that others ran out or did not have. If until the time comes for each one to fend for himself, those who have more do not help those who have less, some will starve while others thrive.

"And I, before nailing my heels forever in this place, I need to know in depth the human and moral quality of each and every one.

"During the arduous journey, we have helped each other without misgivings or material prejudices. When someone fell ill, regardless of their condition, the others multiplied to attend to them when the danger of the Indians has arisen, we have all risked our lives in favor of the community, because we were all one, and when there were unfortunate casualties, Because life is like that, the poorest or richest fallen were buried in the open meadow and we all fell to our knees to pray a prayer for their souls, because all the souls that left among us were equal before God and men.

"But we have reached our goal and this raises the need to assess attitudes. We are going to need all our courage and all that we have left to defend our lives, and I ask those who arrive better gifted than others, if they are willing that this harmony that reigned between us during the trip, will not be broken and that each and every one of us will contribute what we have for the common good.

"This does not mean that the one who has the most should gracefully give it to the one who has the least. It would not be fair and, therefore, whoever gives to someone who lacks, will receive proof of the value of what he has lent, so that, in due time, when the one who received it is in a position to do so, he will return it honestly and, if so it demands, with its corresponding revenues.

"And since I am one of those who can lead by example, because luck helped me earn some money during my years leading caravans and I used it to supply myself for this last trip, I will be the first to make available to the community how much I have.

"The day that is over, it will end for me and for everyone and if we have to go hungry, we will go through it equally.

"But I need the unreserved consent of everyone. If not, here the caravan ends. I will continue to New Mexico, because I have the means to get there and for everyone to manage as best they can.

"This is how much I have to expose before starting to unload my wagons and dedicate myself to building my home; Let others speak, and if they are willing to imitate me, let them swear with their hand on this Bible that I bring, that they will imitate me in everything, because I will know how to set the right example.

"Now you have the floor.

There was no discrepancy. All solemnly swore to help those whose resources were exhausted by pledging to repay what was loaned when they were in a position to do so.

Bird, satisfied by the noble attitude of all who made up the caravan, stopped them saying:

"But this is not enough, comrades. We must prevent ourselves for the future and I want that just as we are going to be united as one in this regard, it is imperative that we be united in other very important ones.

"We all know from bitter experience what human ambitions and selfishness mean in the lands we have left behind. We all know the ambition of those who only seek the good, what already pays off, without having to suffer the bitterness of working to make it perform. You all know of the plunder of cattle thieves, of the desperate, and even of those who, because they possess money, seek what is convenient for them to the detriment of those who possess it.

"We are going to limit many acres of land, we are going to make them flourish, we are going to turn this into a fertile valley that one day may tempt someone's greed and I want to demand two things from everyone.

"One, that, when defending the common heritage, there are no restrictions. We will all have to expose what is necessary, as if we only defend our own; and another, that no one will ever sell anything they now choose as property, to prevent disturbing elements from seeping into us and one day turning into hell what appears to be paradise.

"This does not mean that if someone gets tired one day and wants to retire, they cannot do so or should leave behind what cost them so much sweat. Not that. The idea is that, if this opportunity arises, offer it to the community so that they can buy it.

"If there is no one who wants to take charge of the acquisition alone, they will do it among several, and if not, among all, but everything that we now limit will be ours without interference from strangers.

"And it doesn't matter that over time new settlers arrive who want to settle among us. There will be plenty of land where they can do it, but before they drive a stake into the ground they will have to abide by the covenant that we sign and if they refuse, they will be forced to settle a mile beyond the town limits. We will not admit dangerous wedges that disturb the close harmony that we are going to achieve.

"If you are in agreement with this new point, swear it too and in due course a document will be drawn up containing all the agreed points. Let there be a witness record that can be invoked in its day if someone tries to miss it.

"This document will be the one signed by those who arrive later and want to stay. Thus, no one will claim one day that the commitment did not exist or intends to deform it to their liking.

They all agreed with the old caravanner. They understood that their forecasts were a shield for everyone and that this would protect each other.

After the solemn oath, the terrain was studied and the advisability of settling only on one shore or both was discussed. Victor gave his opinion.

"I understand that in both and thus we will be more crowded and closer to each other. The river, except in times of alluvium, is fordable, but, even so, we can build a bridge that unites us. If we only occupy one shore, tomorrow others may come to settle on the opposite, and if they propose to do so, create difficulties for us.

His proposal was accepted and he went on to study the amount of land that each one would need according to the family that accompanied him and the useful arms that he could use to cultivate it.

It was also agreed that the town should be agglomerated on the southern shore, as it is the most protected and most of the crops would be spread on the opposite shore, except for some plots along the shore in the part of the town. Then, the locations of each settler would be raffled and the town limits would be set.

It was a daunting two-day task, but at the end of this short stage, everything had been planned.

The plots were drawn. Some were closer to the river than others, but the land was fertile everywhere and, if necessary, the opening of channels would be studied to bring water to the lands that needed it.

With the creation of the town, it proceeded to distribute it in the same way. The cabins would surround a large square that would open in the center, leaving a certain amount of free land to eventually found a school, build a small church and when possible, a City Council that would take care of the state and cleanliness of the town, as well as a house for the sheriff, if the town grew and it was necessary to appoint an authority.

But while this came, which would take time, someone needed to assume a Platonic authority to intervene in case of dispute between the colonists. Everything had to be safeguarded, and Victor safeguarded it. It was unanimously agreed to grant him this authority, but Bird flatly refused. He demanded that two more be named and only in case these two did not agree, he with his vote would decide whose reason was.

After all this preliminary work, they all feverishly devoted themselves to building their cabins, which was the most pressing thing for them. Later, when they had their families sheltered from the cold and rain, there was time to start plowing the land.

And so the new town was founded, which one day appeared with a banner nailed to a tree, in which you could read the patronymic with which it should be known. Over time, new settlers were added who when crossing the plain and discovering that new, flourishing, quiet town, wanted to join it, and after accepting the conditions imposed, they settled without any inconvenience.

Until one day, twenty miles from there, the rails of the great railroad that was to unite the nation from East to West and turn it into one of the most ugly regions of the entire State began to set in the land.

But with the railroad the threat had to come that would break the peace and tranquility of its inhabitants. That area, even though it was the poorest in the state, was desirable, because the train would solve many problems and with it in sight, agricultural and livestock expansion would have become irresistible.

CHAPTER II

TWO OLD COMPANIONS

The life of the town could be consolidated two years after it was raised, not without its inhabitants ceasing to suffer countless hardships and deprivation, but solidarity had reigned among them and, helping each other, they managed to get out of the traffic jam.

Until then, the utility extracted from the land had only served to be able to live off their first harvests, but it was not yet possible for them to obtain a greater profit by selling the surplus. There was a long way to go before they could organize a small market where they could sell their products and receive some money to spend on things that were very necessary to replace those they had worn out.

Victor, as a man of the prairies, was worrying about that very pressing problem, he imposed himself to do two very important things: one, to register the limited land to safeguard it from possible debris; another was to visit villages that were relatively close to each other to sell or exchange items that had just provided the settlers with what they needed most.

The search was to be made in Hutchinson, which was the nearest town of importance where the Register was located in that area, and this involved a hundred-mile journey cutting ground.

The other thing that was imposed to do according to the criteria of the former caravanner, was more ambitious, but he had a certain vision for the future and he made it known to the settlers.

The site chosen to settle was a kind of small meadow or tiny valley, sunk between two high depressions in the ground.

The village had been built in the shelter of the eastern depression, which cut off the wind and partly protected them from sandstorms when they proceeded in the direction of the western depression, but they ended in the middle of the small valley. The rest was blue grass, in which the cattle that had been saved from so many vicissitudes, were nourished, sumptuously fattening easily.

Thus, the young that had been born of lambs and goats and even some cattle, also presented a magnificent appearance. If they had the means to acquire more cattle, in a short time it would be easy for them to provide themselves with a valuable herd.

This had been seen in advance by the former caravanner and for this reason, when he had decided to undertake the march to Hutchinson alone, he gathered the settlers and said:

"I have been thinking that since everything we have occupied and put into work so far is going to be recorded, it would be very useful to also record everything that remains of the meadow until the depression that cuts it off.

"It is true that so far it is not useful to us, except to browse the few cattle that were saved from slaughter, but no one can foresee what may happen tomorrow, when we continue to prosper and the railroad helps us solve problems that at the moment they exceed our possibilities of action.

"That ugly piece of grass can be very useful to us in two ways. One, to be able to sell some more plots for the benefit of all if other emigrants arrive and feel the desire to settle here. If we have gone through and endured the worst and those who come will find many difficulties resolved, it is fair that they do not enjoy the same privileges and contribute in money what they were spared from contributing in work and fatigue. It would help us to acquire livestock or things of common utility and it would not diminish the value of our crops.

But there is more. I have heard opinions, projects for the future; Here there are those who before being a colonist were a cowboy and dream of being able to raise a small ranch and raise cattle that report a good profit.

"I know that markets have been opened en route to receive all the cattle that come from Texas and that due to the lack of meat that the war has produced, everything that arrives sells very well. If we could raise cattle we would take advantage of this shortage streak and could sell them more profitably than the ranchers coming up from Texas.

"But for that, it is necessary to ensure pastures and we have pastures. Of course, we could not install a ranch here on a large scale, but one in tune with the possibilities offered by this unexploited piece of land.

"And it is my idea that we also register it as property of the community and when luck helps us a little more, acquire cattle, build the ranch and exploit not only agriculture, but livestock.

"It is an ambitious dream and perhaps not in the short term, possibly I, who am already old, do not see it fully realized, but if I died before achieving it, I would leave the world satisfied that I had contributed to ensuring the well-being of a handful of families. worthy of being helped in all respects.

"This is my idea, you guys study it while I prepare the wagon to go to Hutchinson to check the registration on everyone's behalf. What you agree will be what is done.

One of the settlers made an objection:

"Do you think that is easy? Registering the plots of each one is not complicated, since a plan of the place has been drawn, with the land that each colonist occupies and our names, but ... how would we register the prairie in what remains untapped? In order for the State to grant us the privilege of considering ourselves owners of uncultivated land, it requires the exploitation by whoever requests the registration and we can demonstrate that we each exploit the bounded land, but the prairie ... none of us exploit it and, in the name of who would verify that record?

"Well, on behalf of the entire town. It would be a communal property and, in terms of exploiting it, we can show that we have our livestock in it and that we intend to build a ranch and acquire more roses. I don't think there is any difficulty in getting it, for a reason. What the government wants is that the wealth of the soil increases, that each day the mother earth produces more and if it has to give away that land in exchange for greater productivity, it does not care to whom it is given, but the product that is given. derives from it. We do not want it to continue as it has been up to here, but to make it useful for everyone.

"If you think that is feasible, there is no more to talk about. I have limited myself to pointing out a possible failure, but if it does not exist, go ahead.

"Over there. With the map of the town and the plots in operation, as well as the names of all the owners, we will issue a document signed by them, in which the total award of the piece of meadow is requested to build a ranch and increase even more the cattle we own. I am sure there will be no opposition to it.

"That being the case, we will sign it and hopefully you will grant it to us!

Victor extended the document, put it for everyone's signature and with it the general plan of the meadow, as well as the location of the town, he prepared to leave. Before doing so, he stated:

"Now, if someone has money and doesn't mind using it, they can entrust it to me and I will take advantage of the trip to acquire things that I know are necessary for all of us. We will alleviate many problems that now hinder us. Whoever needs something, give me a list.

When it was time to start the trip, Victor had his pockets full of notes, which he would later have to put in order to find out what he would have to buy in the city.

No one harbored the slightest suspicion that he did not fulfill his promise. First, because he had given many proofs of camaraderie and interest, and second, because he left his fields abandoned, although with the promise of everyone to take care of them in his absence.

Victor made a painful five-day journey to reach the village, but a hardened man on those exhausting routes, he resisted them well, despite not being a child, and entered Hutchinson on the fifth day in the middle of the afternoon. As it was not time to register, since it only worked in the mornings, he looked for an inn where he could sleep that night, to verify the pertinent operations the next day that would leave the matter solved and his companions of fatigue, sure that no one would be able to dispute their land. busy.

When, after leaving the cart at the inn, he took to the street for a walk, he felt strange to everything around him.

Two long years immersed in that abandoned meadow, working like a galley slave and going through hardships like the others, had left Abilene's stamp so deeply etched on his retina that he could not bring himself to the idea of contemplating something so antagonistic as what he was facing. surrounded.

The shops, the streets full of people, the vehicles that circulated, everything that meant dynamism and progress, met there in stark contrast and she did not know whether to feel sorry for not being definitively in that environment, or to yearn more strongly for what had happened. left behind him days before.

And the vision of the small town that surrounded him was stronger in his mind.

That was like a piece of his soul, something that had been born of his effort with him from others; there was nothing frivolous or artificial there; There, everything was intense work, discomfort, sweat, fatigue and deprivation with a view to a more promising future, but there was the welcoming mother earth who deserved such a gift and this had gone so deep into the soul of the former caravanner, that he did not I would have changed for nothing.

It is true that he lacked many necessary things that existed there and that nobody seemed to give them great importance, but with time, they would also have them in Abilene and they would not owe them to anyone, because they would have created them with the effort of their muscles and with sweat of their foreheads.

Perhaps this affection for mother earth was the product of so many years crossing the routes in perennial contact with nature and this had led him to identify with her and love her, despite the fact that she was not always kind and lavish with human beings. .

He, who had crossed so many diverse landscapes, knew that there were good and bad lands, that some offered heat and water to the ears and others frost and hail to scorch them; that, in some places, the sun put flowers in the fields and in others, blizzards and ice that gripped the bodies at the slightest faint, but in the final balance, the mother earth was that: the mother of humanity, because it contributed to their support and everything consisted of knowing how to choose and knowing how to work it.

He was walking in a daze down the main street, when a heavy and rough hand rested on his shoulder and a voice whose timbre was familiar to him exclaimed:

Hell's Bells, Bird ...! You in these lands?

Victor turned to recognize the one who had thus greeted him. It turned out to be a caravanner who had traveled several routes with him before leaving the caravans. It was a guy who was already over thirty-five years old. He was tall, strong, with a determined expression, a very tanned face and a fairly acceptable figure according to the tastes of women.

He wore a plaid shirt, a suede vest, denim trousers, and mid-calf boots topped at the heels by long sliced spurs. His hat was a cowboy, very tall with a crown, wide brims, and with two studied dents in the front of the crown.

Victor remembered him as a tough and resistant pawn, he had always endured the roughness of the road well, although he had always been a somewhat strange man, very sensitive to getting into fights and fights for reasons that were sometimes unimportant.

Victor, smiling, replied:

"Hello Adam. I was not counting on bumping into you in these latitudes either.

"Indeed, it seems that cities like these are not the most frequented places for us, at least until recently, but the wheel of life turns many times and sometimes, places us where we could least imagine we could be.

"But you, who have always been an old wolf of the routes, seem to have abandoned them, is that correct?

"Indeed, Adam, I abandoned them because I am feeling old and that requires strength and youth. I have a few thousand miles on my ribs and I think it was time for me to take over.

"To live on your income, then?

"My income? Don't mock, Adam. You well know that the rents of a caravanner disappear when you finish a route and you have to live off the product until you can undertake another. My income was always poor.

"Then...

"I have become a settler. It is time for me to rest my legs and my ribs and make the most of the days that remain in my life. And what do you do? Did you also abandon the caravans?

"Indeed, Bird. I abandoned them because, like you, I felt tired of traveling through inhospitable lands and exposing my life fighting against the elements and the Indians. One is still young and must bring to life a juice that open landscapes with no other charms than guiding wagons, do not provide.

"I am at the service of a cattle rancher who traffics a lot in cattle and although there are also some fatigue in driving, there are many rest periods to visit cities like this and have fun for a few days, knowing that the salary runs every month and do not wait for new employers to emerge.

"But… we are talking dry and that is not right. We have to celebrate our meeting and I invite you to a whiskey or two, whatever you want to drink.

"Thank you, and I will accept it so as not to snub you, but I will tell you that it has been more than two years since a drop of alcohol has entered my throat.

"Hell's Bells! … Is that possible?

"As I tell you!

"Did he withdraw from drinking? You had a good stomach to assimilate it.

"True, and I will tell you that at first I missed it a lot, but you get used to everything. Where I have spent these last two years, there was only river water and you had to get used to it.

"Well, you will tell me. I'm curious what he's done since we didn't see each other four years ago.

Adam led him to a nearby tavern, where he ordered two glasses of whiskey, and seated at a table they resumed their conversation.

"My life lacks relief", Victor affirmed. On the other hand, yours, as restless and hard as you were, I suppose it will be more interesting than mine.

"Don't believe it. I left the caravans three years ago, after having caught pneumonia that almost took me to hell and then I decided to abandon the routes.

"I worked as a laborer on a farm, later on a ranch and later, through a friend, I became part of the team of a cattle dealer, who buys and sells many cattle throughout the year.

"It does work hard many times, but it pays well and there are always gaps left to have fun and compensate for work.

"So, your income …

"My income goes to whiskey and some good girls with whom I usually spend time in the gambling dens, but I have fun, which I did not do before.

And since this has been my life since we haven't seen each other, now tell me yours, which should be more interesting.

"Interesting to be listened to, perhaps, but to experience it it couldn't have been tougher, although with the hope that it won't take long to receive compensation.

Bird told him how he had joined a caravan of exiles and how they had settled on the shores of Smoky Hill, where they decided to settle and build a town with the poor means they had left.

Víctor related the vicissitudes suffered until he was able to half assure his existence with the product of the crops and as given the imminence of the inauguration of the "Union Pacific", they would have safe means of transport to place their crops and be able to acquire what they needed and did not yet possess. .

Adam, while listening to him, had requested two new glasses of whiskey, and Bird encouraged by the drink to which he was no longer used, ended up explaining to his old companion of fatigue all the projects of the colonists and the reason that had led him to the town.

Adam, who had listened carefully and without interrupting, exclaimed:

"So they own a town with a hundred neighbors and, in addition, a beautiful expanse of prairie?

"We practically are, because we have been working the land for two years. Now I have come precisely to verify the registration of our plots and the part of free pasture. We think, as soon as circumstances allow us, to raise a ranch together, acquire cattle of those that come by the thousands from the part of Texas and found a kind of meat market, covering the nearest towns for several miles around. .

"Nice business, from what I see.

"It may be, but not so soon, Adam. Keep in mind that we are very tight on means and that until we find a way to sell our crops, we will not have any money to start with. Before we have to provide ourselves with many necessary things that we lack, but we are tough and strong and everything will come.

"That registration thing will be very complicated. Being a hundred owners.

"Do not believe it. I bring a perfect plan of the plots, their location and dimensions and the authorizations of all to do the registration on their behalf. As for the prairie, it will be registered as communal property and there will be no inconvenience. On the other hand, you know that, in the case of distant lands, without an owner or symptoms of colonization, the State provides all kinds of facilities. The question is that mother earth is worked, that it produces and that it benefits everyone.

"Well, Bird, you don't know how much I celebrate your good luck... Will you tell me where that town is, in case I ever get the chance to go say hi to you? As I travel a lot in these places with cattle, maybe I spend a day nearby and take the opportunity to take a look at it, to see how it is doing.

"I don't think it will be difficult for you to find it. Just follow the course of Smoky Hill. It is about twenty miles below a town called Victoria, where the railroad is already being built.

"I'll keep that in mind in case I can visit you. And now tell me what you intend to do tonight.

"Nothing, Adam. Since I can't register all these papers until tomorrow, I'll go to bed early.

"Early, when God knows until what other time he will not be able to live among civilized people?

"You will not think that I am like you who are of the age to run partying in style.

"Of course not, but he's not going to become a foodie either. Why don't you accept that we have dinner together? We have had many bad drinks on the roads, we have run common dangers and we have not seen each other for a long time. In case we delay in meeting again, or we do not see each other again, it is only fair that we spend some time in pleasant company and remember times past. I hope you don't look down on me.

Although what Victor wanted was to rest as much as possible from the breakdown of the trip, since he had another day as rough as the one he suffered in perspective, he did not dare to snub his old caravan companion and said:

"Well, Adam, because I am you, I will make an effort, but I assure you that my stamina is no longer what it used to be, and that now my bones suffer more easily and demand rest from me. I will accompany you to dinner, but I will retire soon. Tomorrow after verifying the registration, I have to move a lot to acquire an endless number of things that my colleagues have asked me and immediately start the path of the town. There are a hundred miles of wagon that when the habit of rolling them has been lost, they weigh a lot.

"Agree. Where are you staying?

"In a very modest inn, Adam. You have to be tight with money until the situation changes. The inn is called "Los Tres Sauces", and it is in a square that precisely because it has three willows in it, gives it its name.

"I know where it is. At half past nine I'll look for you in it. Now I have something to do, but by that time I will be free.

"Very good. At half past nine I'll wait for you there.

They said goodbye with a strong handshake and got up. Victor seemed a bit dizzy from the lack of habit of drinking, but he estimated that, with the mid-afternoon air, he would wake up and that by dinner time he would be clear again.

And abandoning Adam, who disappeared down the road, he began to walk unsteadily, breathing eagerly the dry, cutting air that was blowing at that moment.

He would have to be careful to drink little during dinner, to avoid further dizziness.

CHAPTER III

THE FEAT OF AN EVIL

At half past nine, Adam showed up at the inn where Victor was waiting for him at the door.

The inn, as the former caravanner had said, was installed in a not very large square, with little movement, and to go out to a more central and busy street, you had to cross a narrow, dirty and poorly lit alley that connected the street with the square. Adam, smiling, took Victor by the arm and pulled him saying:

"We are going to have dinner in a very typical restaurant, where they serve very good food. I recommend it for when you have to come back here.

"Who knows, when will I do it and if I will return. It is a very hard day to do it often and if the railway is inaugurated soon, it is preferable to go to Victoria and take the train there. Progress is imposed and this of the wagon trains rolling miles and miles down difficult and dangerous paths, will go down in history before long. One day, those of us who were caravanners will be some picturesque pictures to illustrate the tales and stories of our descendants.

Adam led him through various streets that Bird was unfamiliar with, until he stopped in front of a modest restaurant on a secluded and narrow street. It was a regular-sized establishment, where a maximum of two dozen people could eat at the same time.

They took a table in the corner and Adam chose a large menu based on roasted bison hump, bean omelette, potatoes to liven up the hump, and apple pie. He also ordered two bottles of California wine, very popular in those latitudes.

As they dined the conversation became lively. Both recalled stages of their life as caravanners full of anxiety, and Bird, encouraged by the California wine with which he poured the dinner, returned to the theme of his new life as a settler, giving hair and signs of all that they had done and of what they hoped to get around not long.

After dinner that lasted until after eleven o'clock, Adam ordered coffee and two glasses of rum and when they left the restaurant at eleven thirty, Bird felt his stomach heavier than if he had filled it with stones and as for his head, it was a small whirlwind due to the alcohol ingested.

Victor had wanted to pay at least for coffee and rum, but Adam had strongly objected, saying:

"No way. I have invited and no more talk. I want you to have a good memory of this meeting of ours, in case we don't see each other anymore.

"Who knows. The world goes around a lot and you have already seen; when we least suspected it, we have met again.

"You are right, but history does not always repeat itself.

Adam, taking him by the arm, since Victor seemed to hesitate a little, asked:

"What do we do now? We could go for a walk and visit one of those places where good girls perform. We would spend a full evening.

"Thanks, boy, but that time of hanging out with good girls passed for me. I go to bed because I have to get up early to go to the Registry and then visit stores. I have a lot of homework left before I see myself in town again.

"Well, if that is your firm purpose, I don't want to upset you. I will accompany him to the inn and then I will see where I end up doing the digestion.

Always clinging to his arm, they continued on their way to the inn. It was close to twelve o'clock and traffic on the streets was almost nil. Those who had not retired to rest were confined in taverns and gambling dens.

At last they reached the alley that led to the square. Not a soul was passing through it and it was almost dark.

Adam released Victor's arm, saying:

"Be careful not to trip and fall! Get up to the walls, which is the safest thing to do.

Bird, who seemed dizzy, heeded the advice, and leaning one side against the walls, continued walking while Adam, almost next to him, but a little behind, followed him.

Until suddenly, the former caravanner felt a sharp and tremendous pang in his back. The pain forced him to open his mouth to scream, but he did not have time, and as if struck by lightning, he fell sideways next to a shadowy doorway.

Adam coldly tugged at the handle of the knife that he had viciously driven into his former partner's back and bent over him quickly, searching his pockets.

Eagerly he seized everything they contained and with a fast step he left the alley, going out to the immediate street, to lose himself in other streets on the opposite side.

When he was safe, he reached for the light of a lamp hanging from a doorway and eagerly examined everything stolen. There were the plan of the town, its geographical location, the plots of each colonist and the documents signed by all. He had also seized eight hundred dollars that had been given to Victor to make purchases.

The plan that had been drawn since he met Bird and he recklessly informed him of the mission that had led him to Hutchinson, had turned out as he had conceived it and now he only had to see if the stab inflicted on the former caravanner had been successful. as deadly as he had tried. If he was found dead, he would have nothing to fear and the last part of his daring project could be put into practice safely. He would register all the land in his name, including parcels and meadow, and then he was sure to find the person who would buy from him for an amount that he had set, the land registry.

When he had the money in his possession, it would disappear forever from those latitudes and the buyer would deal with the settlers at the time of taking possession of the meadow and demanding the payment of the leases or forcing them to buy them despite being theirs.

The wretched Adam retired to the inn where he was staying, but did not sleep all night. Now he felt the agonizing doubt of not knowing if he had struck Bird down, shutting his mouth forever, or if, despite his spectacular fall, the wound had not been as deadly as his plans demanded; This agonizing doubt forced him to get up early and throw himself into the street aimlessly.

A morbid curiosity prompted him to approach the alley where he looked fearful, but he could see that the bleeding body of the former caravanner was no longer there. Someone must have discovered him dead or injured, withdrawing him from circulation.

Completely nervous, he was walking around until mid-afternoon when the town newspaper went on sale, and feverishly, he acquired a copy, retiring where no one would see him to look for any news that would clarify his situation.

Until, on the last page, he found a leaflet that said:

MYSTERIOUS CRIME

This morning, in an alley that leads to the Plaza de los Sauces, two passers-by who were circulating there discovered the body of a half-bled man, who was lying face down on the ground.

He had a huge wound on his back, produced by a knife, although this was not found near the wounded man. They must have stabbed him by surprise, perhaps to rob him, since no money or any document was found in his clothes to identify the attacked man.

He was taken to the hospital in a desperate state and in the middle of the day, when we have visited the hospital and talked with the doctors, they do not hide their pessimism. They do not have much hope of being able to save his life and less that he can declare something that clarifies the mystery. Even in the unlikely event that your life was saved, it will be many days before you are in a position to testify.

We severely condemn such a disgusting crime, and we urge the authorities once again to increase vigilance in order to avoid such blameworthy events, events that tend to occur too frequently and that discredit the good name of the city.

Adam breathed easy after reading the news. Whether Bird died or was saved, for the moment he was knocked out to thwart his plans and put him in danger. He could calmly attempt the land survey and disappear from there to talk to whoever he was sure would agree to discuss the purchase of that record.

After the operation was carried out and he received the money, he would disappear from that area and the buyer would deal with the settlers. Legally, he would be the owner of the land and no one could complicate the fate of the former caravanner.

The next day he was presented at the Registry with the map of the town and the plots.

He had presented himself very well dressed, as if he were actually a well-off man, and after playing a few jokes with the Registrar to gain his sympathy, he explained the operation in his own way.

He had discovered that land by taking possession of it and had dealt with some caravans to lease them a part of the little valley, which they accepted. They had settled there, they had divided up the land as it could be shown by the plan that he presented and the rest he was going to use to build a small ranch and raise cattle.

The Registry clerk didn't seem very interested in Adam's explanations. His mission was to take note of the place, admit the plan with the approximate indications of the location, and even the name that had been given to the town. The rest was up to the person who registered the property.

And since there were many records that were verified of parcels that the Government gave free to the settlers, the matter did not present complications for the procedures. Later, if the inspectors wanted to make a visit to check if indeed the land registered was in exploitation, that was their mission.

With all the paperwork verified, the registration fees paid, which were modest, and the supporting documents in his pocket, Adam quickly disappeared from Hutchinson. He was there only passing through, and his destination, though not very far away, was quite another.

Adam had told Victor something about his current life, but he had reserved the most interesting. If he had declared it, the former caravanner would have thrown him from his side as an undesirable.

It was true that he worked for a cattle dealer, but not a dealer with whom he could deal decently. His name was Ludwing Swan and he only dealt with cattle thieves, buying from them the product of their plundering at a low price, and then placing it as best he could, with a profit that far exceeded what a legal trade would have yielded him.

The biggest drawback and the most dangerous that plagued him was that he lacked a safe place where he could gather the cattle and camouflage them until they could be released.

This was a problem that made him mad, as he was forced to look for intricate places, far from easy inspection, to store the cattle, always exposed to being discovered at some point.

Adam, who was not unaware of this, was sure that he could deal with Swan about the purchase of that ideal land, since as the absolute owner of the land, he could impose the payment of a rent on the settlers, or sell them their plots and also, he could raise an empirical ranch in the patch of prairie, gather in it as many cattle as he acquired under his status as a trafficker and be protected from so many dangers, since the place, according to Victor had told him, was isolated and it was not easy for anyone to enter nose in business.

Adam went to a town called Sterling, where Swan was now. He had just sold two hundred cattle that had been causing him many headaches, as they had been looking for them so hard and he wanted to find a rest before getting into new complications.

Swan had unleashed the half dozen men in his service. They were all more or less of Adam's moral condition, since they all knew the kind of business their employer did.

Swan, who did not expect to see Adam so soon, greeted him saying:

"How the hell are you here, now, if you've only been gone four days? There is nothing for now.

"I can imagine.

"So what's up? Is it that you have already finished the money and come to ask for more on account? It is too early for that.

"No, don't be alarmed, I don't need any loan. I have enough money to be able to wait as long as possible.

"So what are you coming for?

"To deal with you on business.

"Any new cattle tips? No, not for now. I want to let the sheriffs get tired of searching and I won't buy a single horn for at least a month.

"It is about something more important than all that, Swan, and I hope you will listen to me and think a bit about the proposal that I have come to make you. I talk to you about the matter before anyone else, because it is a duty to do so, since you have helped me to get ahead, but if you are not really interested, there will be nothing lost, because what I have come to offer you and at the price I'm going to give it to you, I have dozens of guys willing to buy it.

"Hmm ...! Since when do you have something to sell that is your property?

"Since two days ago.

"Well, let's see what it is, since you assure me that it interests me so much, and let's see how to justify your ownership.

"This is justified by documents that no one can dispute.

"Well, go ahead; speaks.

"You have a tremendous problem in mind, which is being able to have a suitable place to collect the bundles you buy without anyone being able to snoop in them and give you the necessary peace of mind to be able to wait for the most productive occasions to sell the cattle.

"Well, I come to offer you that place and not only that, but a whole small town, with a hundred settlers settled in it, without having the acquired right to consider themselves the owners, since they did not bother to register the property in due time.

"I offer you that town with its one hundred plots from which you can demand a rental income, or the purchase of them if you prefer, and, in addition, a large piece of meadow near the town, where you can build a ranch that serves as a cover. for your business. It is a magnificent place, on the bank of a river and away from all known routes. It has the advantage that, shortly, when the railway opens, you will have it twenty miles away, which will facilitate the movement of cattle and by doing things as the Devil commands, you will pass in the eyes of all as an honest trader in cattle, because the one that you are established precisely next to a town occupied by a hundred settlers will protect you.

"A nice view", replied Swan, intrigued by Adam's words. Where is this paradise that you offer me located?

"I have no problem telling you, because it is so safe in my hands that no one can take it from me. The town already has a name, Abilene, and is nestled on the shores of Smoky Hill, about twenty miles from Victoria, which is the closest place where the "Union Pacific" will circulate. The small valley is sandwiched between two depressions in the terrain, which protect it and cut off common routes; that is, it is not a place of transit if it is not sought.

"And to convince you, here is a map of the valley, the place occupied by the town, where the plots are located, with the names of the settlers and the piece of meadow where you can build the ranch and have the cattle under cover of glances. indiscreet. For the settlers, you will be the absolute owner of the valley and a decent rancher who trades in cattle.

Swan carefully examined the plans and then said:

"Not bad. Now you will explain the rest to me.

"The rest, what is it?

"How did this get into your hands and how can you prove that it is yours and you can sell it.

"How it came to my hands, is something that does not interest. When you buy cattle from cattle rustlers, you don't ask them where they got them from; You buy them because they interest you and the rest does not count. When you sell them, those who buy them know that they are not acquired honestly, but since they earn with the purchase, they acquire them without asking more questions and this is my case.

"As for my right to offer it to someone, it is here very clear. This is the land ownership registry with everything it contains and you know the records well enough to know that it is legal and that no one can challenge it.

Swan, increasingly intrigued, studied the documents and convinced of their legality, he said;

"Why don't you exploit it?

"For two reasons. One, because I would need money that I don't have to settle there; and another, because ... it is better that once sold, it disappears. It is possible that someone does not agree with being required to pay a rent of what they believe is theirs and try to make arrangements to clarify why the land is registered in my name. I would be in a hurry to give explanations and it does not suit me. But legally sold and being you a buyer, not the one who registered the property, no one can ask you for accounts. You have legally bought it from whoever presented legal documents to sell it and you don't know more.

"In effect, this endorsement would protect you from those explanations that you apparently could not give. The person in charge of the registry would be you and I would have nothing to know about him, since, when buying the land, I would do it with irrefutable documents at sight, but you will not deny me that, for the moment, I would be very besieged to give to my time explanations of how I acquired it and to whom.

"To whom is clear, since my name is on the registration document. With saying that I offered it to you, you studied it, it seemed good to you and you acquired it, business concluded. You didn't have to know how it came to me.

"Later, if they are interested, let them look for me. I will disappear from here marching very far, and the fait accompli are the ones that count.

"Indeed, but think that at least until the tide calms down and those people have to resign themselves to knowing that the owners of the plots are not them but me, they are going to keep me in check and I will not be able to dedicate myself with tranquility to my business.

"That can last a month or at most two. When all their efforts are exhausted and they are convinced that nothing has a solution for them, they will have to resign themselves and agree with you.You can be magnanimous with them, affirm that you have bought in good faith, that you know nothing about the background of the matter and that you are willing to let them continue in their plots. They will finish by thanking you for your behavior and everything will return to the most complete calm. What you lose from earning in a business during this time, you will compensate with the rents you get from the plots or the sale of them if it suits you. Don't start putting Chinese on the trail because the path is very clear.

"Well, it is possible, but I will have to study it. What do you ask for the transfer of these rights?

"Ten thousand dollars.

"Doesn't that seem like a lot of money for the complications that the purchase can provide?

"The complications are minimal, the profit is very profitable and if in reality this had not come to my hands through a slightly crooked path and I would have been the true discoverer of the land, I would not sell it twice. I have to lose and win, precisely because the only one who could not exploit this without difficulty would be me.

"Ten thousand dollars is crap for what it is worth and if it does not suit you, you leave it and I will look for another buyer, but I warn you not to think about reducing a single dollar, because I will not admit it. I have put in my accounts and that is the money I need.

"It's okay, Adam. I would like to know something about how you managed this poker play with all the aces in your favor.

"I repeat that this is my thing. You study if you accept it or not and I give you time until tomorrow at this time to answer.

"I will study it and tomorrow we will meet again. The thing is still not very clear and I must weigh the pros and cons.

Swan took those twenty-four hours to study the proposition thoroughly. The fact that Adam had not wanted to give any details of how he had seized those plans and how he had been able to search the land in his name, had suspected that the procedures used had not been very orthodox. Perhaps someone who was going to verify the registry had paid with his life for the consequences of a confidentiality of that nature and then, it was understandable that those who had entrusted their representative with the failed mission of verifying the registry, should take all kinds of steps to put into effect clear the plunder. But this did not affect him in the end. If he legally acquired the valley before a notary public and the registration sheet that accredited Adam as legal owner was attached to the deed, to look for him and ask him for an account of his performance. He would come out free of all suspicion, since he would buy "in good faith" what they offered him with reliable documents.

And understanding that the business was magnificent, he accepted. He knew that he would have to fight many dialectical battles with the colonists until he reduced them to the reality of the situation and the rest mattered little to him.

When everything calmed down, he would build the ranch and it would be there where the acquired bundles would find a legal refuge, something that until that moment had been impossible to obtain.

What time would bring him later, he would see how he weathered it.

CHAPTER IV

AN INQUETING ABSENCE

In the absence of Victor, who was the strong man of the town, who resolved small conflicts and was always ready to help whoever needed it, one of the two settlers who were appointed with Bird had been substituted for him to settle any controversy that might arise between the settled. This was Leslie Simpson, a sturdy farmer in his thirties, hard for work, sharp wit to solve "problems" that sometimes arose and that others, less educated, did not know how to solve and a dynamic and friendly man, whom all appreciated for his excellent humane conditions.

Leslie would have stayed in Kentucky where he was not doing badly at all, if Valentine Marqueand, another settler less fortunate than himself, had not decided to undertake the adventure of searching for unknown lands, in a logical desire to overcome a miserable life that had been dragging on for some time. weather.

That Valentine personally decided such a thing would not have mattered much to Leslie, but it so happened that, when Valentine left, he took his daughter Margaret with him, and this did matter to Leslie, for he was in love with the girl. and his purpose was to marry her when circumstances permitted.

Margaret loved the settler, but she couldn't allow her father to have the adventure alone. It was the only thing the old settler had in the world and it was his duty to watch over him.

Leslie had offered Margaret's father to take him into his small estate when he married his daughter, but Valentine had the pride of knowing that he could still fend for himself. He wanted more than the misery he enjoyed, not for himself but for his daughter.

Leslie's reasoning to convince him to accept her offer was useless. The stubborn old man rejected it saying:

"Very pleased that my daughter is marrying you and staying by your side, I know that you really love each other and that she will be happy with you, therefore, you can do it and I will run the adventure to see what I get. It has gotten into my head that towards western Kansas I can find a productive corner to end my days, which I did not achieve here, and I can try it myself.

Margaret, anguished, fought fiercely to harmonize the well-being of the three. He saw himself between a rock and a hard place, between two different loves, but one as deep as the other. She could not renounce Leslie's affection, but neither did her duty as a daughter allow her to leave her father abandoned in that adventure that no one knew how could end.

The only solution that the old settler found was one and he proposed it:

"Since my daughter does not want to abandon me and it is not fair that she renounce her future happiness, I propose something to you. She and I left for the West of Kansas. If I find something much better than what you and I have, I will advise you to get rid of this and come settle with us. You can get married there and we will all live better than we have lived up to now, because, although you enjoy a somewhat better position than mine, it is not so bright that it shelters you from worries. You know well that a lousy one-year harvest would put you in a distressing position for many seasons.

And if I fail and that is no better than this, then I promise to come back here and give up being something other than what I am. I take a year to try the test,

The solution was relatively acceptable, but it didn't suit Leslie either. He knew what it meant for an old man, even if he was still strong, and for a girl like Margaret, the unknown of that journey through lands that still offered innumerable dangers and he could not leave her at the mercy of her father's diminished strength.

And he opted for an intermediate solution. He would sell his property, use whatever money he could earn to equip a good wagon, and go with Valentine and his daughter to the same fate. Whatever was theirs, would be his, and who knew if the old man was right and in the end they would find something more beneficial for everyone in those lands, still almost virgin in many miles of extension.

Margaret was relieved by her boyfriend's decision. That way they would not separate and enjoy the emotions of something that was completely unknown to her, since she had never left the limits of the place where she had been born.

He quickly sold his land. It was not a capital that they were given for them, but it was enough to charter two wagons, load them with food and some domestic animals such as several chickens, a goat and a pig and be able to undertake the journey with great stresses. They still had some money left over to buy some essentials in the future.

Leslie, who had never appeared in any caravan, was almost like an expert of the prairies, to the point that the old Bird not only became very fond of him, but also entrusted him with many essential missions to better ensure the success of the campaign. business.

Leslie had kept her horse, a pretty good and tough animal; In it he made discoveries in front of the caravan, to exploit the terrain and make sure that the road did not offer insurmountable obstacles.

And he was the one who one afternoon discovered a small group of Indians who, ambushed at the top of a hill, were attentively following the march of the carts, with the intention of falling on them when they camped and seizing the loot.

His keen gaze had discovered certain luminous reflections that started from the top of the hill; they were as if a child were playing with a piece of mirror placed in the sun, to send the light beam from a distance.

When he informed Victor of the discovery, the caravanner immediately translated into reality what those signs meant. An Indian spy was communicating with other hidden companions below the hill, to inform them of what he was seeing.

The caravanner was not disturbed, on the contrary, serene and hard, he continued walking in front of the wagons until he found a suitable place to camp. He did it next to a bank that would protect them from behind, while the carts by strict order, formed a compact wheel with the cattle inside, to protect them from the arrows of the Indians, while the men of the caravan took positions in the carts and even below them, rifles at the ready and ammunition close at hand.

It was a nervous night for everyone, particularly the women, who were not allowed to occupy the wagons. In the gap that formed the circle, they spread their duffel bags and there they spent the night under cover of the contingencies that might arise.

But it was close to dawn and nothing had happened. Some emigrants began to question the threat of the Indians. If true, they had had time to attack them since Leslie had discovered the signs.

But Victor, sternly, indicated:

"When you spend a dozen years driving wagons across the prairie, you will learn many things that you do not know. They have not attacked us because the Indians only do it at dusk or dawn, but never in full darkness unless they are very sure of success.

"Therefore, do not be overconfident, as we do not know the number of enemies that can attack us. Think of yours that you can only protect and if there is need, burn your hands with the barrel of the rifles, but do not stop firing viciously.

Victor's warnings had not been his fantasies, as the daylight was just beginning, an impressive scream tore the silence that reigned in the meadow and a chorus of guttural screams was the echo of the scream.

Out of the tall grass, like snakes rising from the ground, emerged as many as two dozen painted Indians, semi-naked, with very high bows adorned with feathers of various colors. Sharp hatchets were carried around their waists in buffalo-skin belts, and, in their hands, the rude and heavy bows, with spare arrows on their backs in quivers woven from strips of lianas.

A rain of arrows fell on the covered wagons, nailing them with a sinister swaying, but the caravanners, complying with the guide's instructions, made their rifles work without giving themselves a break and a curtain of projectiles swept the entire front occupied by the Indians, who all running they tried to reach the cars to take them to the assault.

The retaliation of the emigrants was tragic. Although not all of them were skilled marksmen and others did not manage to keep their pulse calm to set the target, as the battle front was limited, the projectiles reached deadly to the mass of savages and they began to fall, riddled with bullets, without giving them time to kill. reach the wagons.

The mortality suffered in a few minutes forced them to hesitate and retreat, without stopping firing, while another dozen Indians who had remained in the rear. Perhaps taking care of the horses, they came to the aid of their companions, but as they soon understood that the attempt was useless, since the caravan was nourished and made up of tough men, ready to die killing, they hastened to pull the fallen, dragging them through the grass to Ride them on the horses and escape with the bloody load.

Rarely did an Indian leave the body of a companion abandoned; they risked their lives to rescue his corpse and did not give up until they did.

When the last fallen had been collected, protecting the operation, those who were still standing, they began to escape and Leslie, fired by the fight, cried out:

"For them...! We must end that horde!

Enraged, he lifted one of the carts to make way and leaping to his horse that was next to him, he launched himself after the fugitives, believing that the other caravans who had mounts would imitate him, but Victor with great shouts ordered that no one commit such madness, because some could fall into an ambush.

But the notice for Leslie was late. The latter had launched himself first after the Redskins and was pursuing them at a distance.

But when he turned his head and saw that no one was following him, he hesitated and decided to retreat.

But at that moment, he discovered an Indian who, when his horse tripped against some stones, had thrown him by the head from a distance, while the little horse got up and continued his swift race.

The Indian scrambled on the ground looking for the bow that had slipped from his grasp, but Leslie, realizing that the savage was easy prey for him, raised his rifle and fired.

The Indian turned several times on the ground and was grotesquely crouched. Leslie advanced with the horse and, realizing that the savage was dying, leaped from his mount, threw himself on the bow and arrows, tore the hatchet from his waist and swiftly returned to the camp. When several settlers, led by Victor, had organized a relief column, fearing that the brave emigrant had been the victim of their impetus. The joy of all was immense when they saw him reappear carrying those trophies won at so little cost.

However, Victor got angry with him saying:

"He has been reckless and it could cost him his hair. The Indians usually simulate retreats to entrust their enemies and attract them where all the advantages are on their side.

Leslie apologized.

"I thought the others would follow me. If I know not, I wouldn't have galloped after them.

"When I realized it and was about to turn around, a savage fell from his horse to the ground. So I decided to shoot him and when I saw that he had been mortally wounded, I jumped to the ground, and seized his weapons.

And he showed her proud of her feat.

"You lack the hair of the Indian, Leslie" pointed out one.

"I am not as savage as they are to scalpel anyone. Let her go to Hell with her bow and feathers.

When they returned to the wagons, Margaret, very frightened, berated Leslie for his recklessness, but Leslie tried to downplay the matter. It had been a symbolic persecution and if it was true that he was able to get those trophies, it was because fate had so arranged.

This had been the most dangerous adventure they had taken during the trip, for they were not disturbed by the Redskins again.

Leslie had lovingly preserved those trophies, and when she built her hut, the bow and arrows were nailed to the wall, while her sharp hatchet was always hanging from her waist on the opposite side of her Colt.

It was a very useful weapon because it was manageable and threatening, because its edge cut a branch in the air.

This brave caravanner had been one of the most prominent in the town and everyone appreciated and respected him because they also knew him to be a brave man, a generous and helpful guy, always ready to help those in need.

For this reason he had been chosen to govern the town together with Victor and another very skilled settler in the art of hunting beasts. The three of them made up a very comprehensive safety committee.

When Bird was absent, Leslie assumed the responsibility of taking care of order and attending to any unforeseen needs, but life in the village continued to develop meekly, without friction or incidents that required severe intervention.

Leslie was one of those who helped tend the former caravan's crops and he would not notice at all that he had been absent from his property.

In the afternoons, when the work was done and the settlers left their fields to meet in the village, Leslie took advantage of the time to sit on a stone at the door of the hut they had built for Margaret and her father and there they chatted and exchanged impressions about the future.

Two years had elapsed since they arrived in the new town and the wedding was lengthening, without apparently things being arranged to bless the marriage. The town still lacked a church and the distance that separated them from other towns was great.

"How many do you think will be able to solve what is missing so that we can finally get married? Margaret asked.

"I don't think it will be long now, my dear," he said, smiling. We have already talked about that with Victor and we have agreed that when he returns from Hutchinson and our properties are insured, we will build together a small church and we will see how to bring a pastor who takes care of this spiritually. We have wheat stored from the previous harvest and when we collect the current one, there will be plenty to make an exploration trip that allows us to place our products and have money to buy things that are very necessary. If our wedding is to be the first to be held in this town, I want it to be fondly remembered by everyone. Who has passed the worst, may well hope to pass the least bad.

"Victor has calculated about fifteen days between going and coming back and leaving everything solved. When I return, we will discuss some matters that are worthwhile and if everything goes as it is now, I trust that when we harvest the harvest, we can get married. You see that it won't be long.

When the end of the second week passed, the date on which the former caravanner was to be back, everyone was watching the bank of the river where they expected to see him appear at any moment, with the cart loaded with articles that many were essential.

But one day and another, and so on, half a dozen went by, without Victor showing any signs of life, and the settlers began to be alarmed and to make all kinds of conjectures to explain this alarming delay.

Faced with the unusualness of the case, all the men of the town met on the first Sunday in the square, summoned by Leslie. The situation was very strange and it was necessary to make a determination.

The colonist, taking the floor, said:

"This is quite strange and, for my part, I cannot find a correct explanation.

"Bird's calculations were well done. He supposed to spend five days on the trip, but extended one more date for each day, in anticipation of unforeseen delays.

"Accepted that the double trip would consume twelve days, let's put one to verify the registration and two to get the acquisition of all the orders. Added the dates, they are the fifteen days foreseen.

"But six more have passed on them and this is already alarming.

"No one can doubt Bird's honesty: first, for having shown it; second, because the value of what you have left here is much higher than the money we give you for purchases, therefore, a desertion of yours must be firmly discarded.

"And if we eliminate this, we only have the disturbing suspicion that he may have suffered an accident, or perhaps a robbery on the road to strip him of what he was driving.

"This is overwhelming, first because our partner's life is worth more than everything he could bear and second, because it leaves us mired in concern, not only about what may have happened to him, but how and when.

"If it has been on the return, there is no doubt that he will have legally verified the records and that we do not have to suffer concerns about them, but if the accident or attack has been consummated before, what situation is ours and where are they? our properties?

"Until now no one knows about this and there was no fear for what could happen regarding the property; But we cannot forget that he carried the plans and all the necessary documentation to verify the registration and that if all this data had fallen into unscrupulous hands, someone could get ahead of us and register everything in his name, leaving us at the mercy of the prey of any bastard.

And this is what should concern us. These are two unsettling things, both when it comes to Bird's life and our properties.

"And I ask everyone, what can and should be done to clarify what happened?

Someone came forward to say:

"We think the thing is clear, Leslie. Someone has to go to Hutchinson to find out what happened and see if they find out what happened to Bird and what happened to the record.

"Yes; That seems like the right thing to do.

"But the question is who is going to go.

"That's what I ask, who is going to go.

"The mission is thorny, we understand it" continued the one who had advanced to speak, "but Bird being absent, we believe that no one is better suited than you to carry out that mission.

"You do me a great honor by pointing me out as the most suitable, but we must take into account not only the danger to run if there is danger, because that does not scare me much, but my interests and other more intimate things. I would have to leave my lands abandoned at a time when they have to be cared for more eagerly and I must think that I would have to leave here a woman who has spent three years counting day by day the time until we get married and that if something happened to me inevitably, it would be left to its own devices. It is not for me, but for her that I fear.

"It is true, but ... Margaret is not alone, because she has her father. We can swear to take care of your crops indefinitely, if something happens to you with which you will not be abandoned. It is true that he can lose you, which would not be paid for with anything, but think about the situation. If someone takes advantage of an accident suffered by Bird and seizes the documentation to register this in his name, you, us, your fiancée and your future father-in-law, we would be in a worse situation than when we arrived here and life for all would be Hell. They could throw us out of here legally, and what would we do then, having to abandon everything that has cost us a lot of sweat to lift?

"I know that you will have reason to say that what we ask of you, we can ask anyone else with the same right, but not all of us are valid for certain missions. Digging the earth, watering it, reaping the spikes and collecting them is done by anyone, no matter how few lights they have, solving certain matters that require a certain illustration and an appropriate character to achieve it, is not available to everyone. If it were a question of going in search of someone determined to put the revolver to his chest and shoot him, I would offer myself right now, because I have plenty of courage to do so.

Leslie was silent. The colonist's reasoning was not without logic. The matter could be dramatically complicated and not everyone had the appropriate conditions to try to solve it.

And since his instinct to preserve his heritage was stronger than his personal fear, since he gauged what it might mean for his future to be stripped of his property, he made a decisive decision. He would take charge of such a mission and that luck would watch over him.

"Okay" he said. I will make the sacrifice for everyone, but I hope that each and every one of you will be loyal to the promise and that in my absence you will look after my interests as well as your own. As for the future, if something irreparable happens to me, I also trust that my fiancée and my future father-in-law will not be abandoned.

"We solemnly swear that this will not happen. We all agree?

The colonists with their arms raised, swore to fulfill their promise and Leslie set out to undertake the trip to Hutchinson, to investigate what could have happened to Bird and in what state the registry of his properties was.

Margaret shouted to heaven when she learned of the decision made by her fiancé, but he was firm in her, replied:

"He thinks that Bird did the same for everyone and that if he has failed in his endeavor, and has even suffered something irreparable, someone has to follow in his footsteps and resolve this matter. If something can be done for a man like that, you have to try. On the other hand, think what would become of us if we crossed our arms and allowed someone to graciously seize what is very ours. I could not live with the anxiety of not knowing if I step on my own land or am on loan and at any moment they can throw me out of here like a usurper.

"I believe that Bird has simply suffered an accident, but we must try to clarify it, and at the same time, clarify if it was before or after verifying the record.

"I will not travel by wagon like him, but on horseback. This has two advantages; one, that the cart will not incite desires of prey because it does not exist; another, that on horseback I can move more freely and even make the trip in less time than Bird.

"Of course, maybe the time you gain on the trip will be lost in efforts to find out what happened, but it will not be wasted time, quite the opposite.

"I will bring provisions for the trip and since I still have some money left, I will take it for the expenses that I may have during my stay there. I hope I have enough to acquire a beautiful bracelet that you can wear the day we get married.

Margaret had to resign herself to letting her fiancé go, and he set out the next morning. The settler, seized with strange forebodings, traveled in torment, thinking of the energetic Bird. He would regret with all his soul that something irreparable had happened to the old former caravanner, just to help legalize the interests of his companions.

CHAPTER V

LESLIE GETS A SURPRISE

Tired, extremely fatigued and gloomy, Leslie reached Hutchinson in the scheduled five days. He had worked daily journeys of about twenty-five miles to buy time in case this gain could be of any use to him.

He arrived in the middle of the afternoon and since the Registry did not work until the morning, he took advantage of the time to take a well-deserved rest. Perhaps later it would lack business hours to rest.

In the morning, after breakfast, he left the inn and asked where the Registry offices were. He did not know the town and someone had to guide him. As he made his way to the destination, he watched everything unfold before his eyes. He had lost the habit of moving in populated and widespread places and he considered himself a castaway in such a large place.

At the door he stopped to meditate. According to his calculations, it must have been about eighteen days since Bird had to have verified the record. As it was May 8, the visit had to be made on April 20. There was no one at the Registry window and, approaching the employee, he said:

"Excuse me if I bother you, but necessity compels me to inquire if a record of land ownership has been verified here on the banks of Smoky Hill.

"Tell me the name of the person in charge of verifying the registration and the date of the registration.

"The date had to be from April 20 to 22 and the person in charge of verifying it is called Victor Bird, but not precisely in his name, but in the name of a community of one hundred settlers who are the ones who settled there.

"He had a plan with the distribution of parcels, the names of the beneficiaries, and even the name of the town called Abilene. Perhaps this name and the fact that there are so many settlers settled, it would make him remember.

"Indeed, the name of that town sounds familiar to me, but what I don't remember is having verified such a voluminous series of records. Wait anyway and I'll consult the books.

He was looking for data on the dates given by Leslie, while the latter, with his heart in his fist, eagerly followed the maneuvers of the Registrar. The fact that he remembered the name of the village, but had not inscribed as many names, alarmed him.

Finally, the clerk, showing him a voluminous book containing the verified records, exclaimed:

"Indeed, here it is. The inscription was verified on April 21 at 10:40 in the morning, the place is indicated in an attached map, where the settlements' settlement plots, the name of the town, which is the one that you have given me. and some other detail, such as a piece of unexploited prairie destined to build a ranch, but the registry is neither in the name of that Mr. Bird that you indicate, nor that of the settlers settled on the land. The record was verified in the name of Adam Greene, as you can see.

Leslie felt as if a huge mountain had slammed down on his head, leaving him stunned. He would have expected everything except that huge blow that turned into a tremendous reality the fear he had been harboring since Bird stopped showing up on the scheduled date.

"Are you saying that ... the record is made in the name of ... that individual only and that the settlers settled in the village are not listed there at all?

"That's right, sir. He seems very puzzled.

"Missed is not the right word, sir. It is something deeper that lights a bonfire of anger in my chest that I don't know how I'm going to vent. Because that record that you have established in good faith is the product of unspeakable theft and who knows if of a cowardly murder. The person in charge of verifying the registry was the one I mentioned earlier and not in his name, but that of all the settlers. What he tells me makes me fear that someone found out about the object of his trip and in one way or another, managed to eliminate him by seizing all the plans to register the land in his name and become the owner of it.

"But if this is the case, he will have to show his face and when he does, I am afraid that he will have a few hours to live to enjoy the product of his prey.

"And since I can prove what I am saying at any time, I will be grateful if you could tell me what can be done to invalidate that record and put things in proper order.

"Oh, you ask me something that I consider impossible! Here is recorded what each one presents, justifying that the registered land exists and is located in the place that is designated. The registry does not have to know if it really belongs to the one who is presented or to another, since being unregistered, it is property like the mines, of the first who makes the inscription.

"Now, if, as you suggest, the person in charge of verifying this registry was attacked and robbed or murdered and the crime is proven and the author is captured and he confesses, then the authorities are called to issue a ruling on which we would attend. If a judge ruled that there was proven usurpation and that the registration should be annulled and adjudicated to another, we would abide by the provisions of the authority, but only in that way.

"So, if you believe that things happened in a criminal way, report the case to the sheriff, investigate, find the victim and the usurper and have the authority open the corresponding file and issue its ruling. We can not do anything that is justified here, without a higher order.

Leslie, reacting, replied:

"Well thank you very much. I have come to clear up this matter and I will not return to the village without succeeding, even if I have to remove all the land in Kansas. The scoundrel who eliminated our partner Bird and appropriated this, will not enjoy his robbery much.

And desperate, he left the Registry offices.

From that moment on, exhausting work was imposed to clarify what had happened. He needed to know what had happened to Bird, how such a thing could have happened and, furthermore, to locate the rogue who, due to circumstances unknown to him, had found out what was happening on the banks of the river and had taken advantage of it to search the terrain in your name.

And since he understood that the first thing that had to be done was to give legal status to the complaint, not only so that they would look for the impersonator but to be able to know something about the whereabouts of the unfortunate Bird, he went to the sheriff's offices, to report the event now. File the complaint so that the wheel of authority began to turn rapidly.

The sheriff was a fat man, more than middle age, with a red face, unruly gray hair, and a thorny mustache, which gave the impression of having placed a narrow, rough brush under his nose.

But he was a welcoming and friendly man, widely credited in the village for his efficiency and sagacity.

He received Leslie with all courtesy and he, after begging him for attention for the long story he was going to do, gave the star man a record of the entire odyssey suffered by the emigrants, until he managed to raise that town on the shores of Smoky Hill, town that according to what he had just learned, an unscrupulous rogue had appropriated, by usurpation of all the data that Bird carried to make the registration.

When he finished his story, he added:

"Now I think that what is imposed in the first place is to inquire to see what has happened to our colleague. I am justified in fear that he had to be assassinated to prevent him from revolting against the looting and endangering the rogue who stole the papers. Understand that if it had only been a robbery, Bird would have been on the campaign to intercept the thief and none of this has happened. He did not appear in the town despite the fact that a long time has passed, and in the Registry, the first news they have had of this impersonation has been through me a while ago.

The sheriff, who had listened to him with deep attention, replied:

"I also believe like you that your partner was murdered to steal his papers and be able to carry out the search, but where and how? Before reaching Hutchinson or after?

"If it was before, anyone knows in what place, mediating more than a hundred miles from his point of departure to our town, and if it was here ... it is shocking that his body was not discovered, although it could well be that he had hidden it somewhere in the wild difficult to register.

"And I wonder what I can do in this case. There is not the slightest clue to locate your partner and without something tangible to lean on to act, how do I carry out any management?

"You could do something and excuse me if you allow me to give you my opinion.

"On the contrary. Any help I receive I will appreciate it, because I am not so conceited that I believe that what does not occur to me cannot occur to someone else.

"In that case, I will tell you that I see two starting points.

Let's see which ones.

"One is to find out who this guy named Adam Greene is. It is not an entelechy, you have verified the record and you have been here, you may still be or someone may know you. I suspect that a man of such moral condition can be known above all in the gambling dens and houses of a low grade. They are undesirable who live in that environment, because in any other they would not be comfortable.

"I can send my commissioners to take steps in those places that you indicate, but, Mr. Simpson, there is something that does not enter my head and what you a little upset by the news have not noticed without a doubt.

"The fact that?

"Knowing for sure that the Registry did it by means of a usurpation of documents, do not you think of the stupid kind, that it appears to take possession of the land being sure that it would be received with nails and teeth and even more, than by demanding that it demonstrate How have you been able to verify the record, were you charged with murder if you killed your partner to steal his papers?

"Indeed, Sheriff, I have thought about that and the truth is that I do not understand the game. If it were an abandoned land, without inhabiting by anyone, it might be feasible for him to take possession of it without danger, but facing a hundred scammed men who would fall on it like hungry wolves, I consider it unspeakable stupidity.

"Or perhaps a very subtle cleverness, Mr. Simpson.

"Why?

"Well ... because I can think of something that can prove it. If he is not a cretin, he must have realized the danger to run and, therefore, the impossibility of appropriating those lands without risk. In this case, you have a perfect outlet to shake off that danger and avoid it.

"Which one?

"Sell the land to a third party, even if it is for a negligible value than it owns. Sold, you pocket the money and disappear from the scene leaving the buyer in front of you.

"And if he has done so, if the sale has been made legally, based on the registration certificate, the acquirer is free of all blame and nothing can be done against him. He bought in good faith and is the legal owner of the land, without having intervened in the theft of the papers or in the death of his partner, if he was murdered.

"And in this case, he will shake off all responsibility by telling you that, if there was theft, you clarify it and prosecute whoever committed it, since he legally bought and paid what they asked for the transfer of those rights.

Leslie, tense, replied:

"How can you find that out? Admitting that you are correct, any transfer of ownership has to go back to the Registry to change ownership, or otherwise, what was sold would continue to be the property of the seller for legal purposes.

"True, and presumably, if you gave it to a third party and they bought it in good faith, you have rushed to register the land in your name. We can go back to the Registry and inquire to see if there was a change of owner.

"And if there was, things will get even more complicated, because no one will be able to take away your property, unless the rogue who committed the theft is caught and he declares how the documentation came into his hands. Only then could the first be challenged by prosecuting the thief twice, since he stole from you and defrauded the buyer.

"So that we will try to clarify. Now tell me what is the other clue that you were going to point out.

"Well you see, Bird came with a cart to take some items that he was supposed to buy here. If the event happened in Hutchinson, the wagon must have been abandoned somewhere and it would be known from it if it was here or was attacked before it arrived.

"The suggestion seems right to me and I will immediately take care of sending inquiries to the inns in the town, and even to the outskirts, in case they find the abandoned cart. If we locate it, it would be a common thread that takes us further and illuminates this dark matter.

"And since I was very interested in your story, let's see if we can clear up the darkness a bit as quickly as possible.

"Wait for me a moment while I instruct my commissioners to begin investigating the whereabouts of the cart. Then you and I will go back to the Registry to see if you can give us more details there.

"I am very grateful for your interest, Sheriff, and I thank you not only on my behalf, but on that of all my colleagues, who at this moment are with their souls in a thread thinking about what could happen to Bird And what for them would mean that after two years of giving blood on mother earth, a rogue would come or whoever is not, but for that matter it is the same, and deprives them of what is very much theirs.

"And I am very afraid of what may happen, because neither they nor I are willing to be victims of dispossession. This would become a tragic battlefield, as one can imagine what would be a hundred enraged men, ready to defend their land tooth and nail.

"I take charge and we will see what can be done to clear up this mess and return the waters to their legal channels.

He left the office to give orders to one of his commissioners who was sunbathing outside the offices and returned to Leslie, saying:

"It is twelve o'clock; We still have time to get to the Registry before they close; go?

"I'm at your service.

They headed to the Registry. As they approached the window, the clerk greeted the star man warmly:

"Hi Sheriff, how are you around here?

"I come to see if you clarify an apparently very ugly matter, which has occurred on the occasion of the registration of some land next to Smoky Hill.

"Oh yeah! Now that I look at his companion I remember him and I am glad that you have come because, reviewing the books, I have found something that is related to that record.

"Yes? Let's see what it is.

"Simply a change of ownership. On the 24th, an individual named Ludwing Swan, a cattle dealer, with residence in a town called Sterling, appeared here to register in his name the property of the town called Abilene, with all the surrounding land according to the original plans deposited here. He brought the notarized copy of the acquisition deed and the new property was registered in accordance with the Law.

"I have remembered it by the name of the town, since most of the lands that come to the registry are virgin and do not have a proper name.

The sheriff examined the inscription and turning to Leslie who was red with anger, said:

"Do you realize that the rogue was not stupid, but too smart a guy? He knew that he was in serious danger trying to claim the land for himself and he preferred to give it to someone else, albeit with less profit. See here; He has yielded it for ten thousand dollars.

"There will be scoundrel ...! But, if that is worth twenty times more!

"For you, yes, but not for him. Ten thousand dollars is safe money, the other ... was to expose yourself to receiving its weight in molten lead.

"Well, we have already clarified something, although instead of simplifying the matter what it does is complicate it more. The buyer will not resign himself to renouncing his acquisition or even paying him what he has paid for the land, and if things do not roll very well to allow the cancellation of the registration, they will have to understand them with the new owner, Whom for the moment the Law protects. Later ... God will tell.

They left the Registry. Leslie seemed stunned, fearing that the time would come when he would have to return to the village to inform his companions of the tragedy that lay upon them and, even more, he feared what might happen when the legal owner of the land presented itself to him. to throw them out of their fields, or to impose a canon on them at will, which would reduce to a great extent the poor profits that they had managed to collect up to now.

On the other hand, the memory of Bird was not leaving his imagination. A sensitive man, he realized that the unhappy former caravanner had been an innocent victim, sacrificed for the sake of having wanted to render a valuable service to his fellow exodus.

Already at the door of the offices, the sheriff stopped saying:

"As you will see, at the moment no more can be done. We will have to wait for my commissioners to make inquiries to see if they discover the cart or any detail that proves that his partner was here and it was here that they stripped him of the plans. I do not have much confidence in this, because had he been killed here, his body would have been found and we have not found any unidentified dead.

"I think a new management could be tried.

"Which one?

"Find out who that dealer is who bought the property from Greene, to see what clue he can give us regarding the guy he dealt with to buy it. You have to surely know him and know something about him.

"You are right and since the town is not very far from here, I am going to send you a summons to appear. We will see what you can tell us that is of interest. Now let me know where you are staying so I can let you know if I discover something worthwhile.

Leslie gave him the address of the inn, which was located not far from the offices, and the two of them shook hands warmly.

"I'm very grateful for your interest, Sheriff," said Leslie.

"I am simply fulfilling my duty and hopefully luck will be with us and we can locate that buharro. He would regret that this could not be solved, for his colleagues. I take care of what it may mean for them to be deprived of their properties.

CHAPTER VI

A FARM IS JUSTIFIED

Shortly before dinner time, Leslie received a notice from the sheriff to report to the offices, and the anxious settler rushed to the appointment.

The sheriff, very serious, said:

"We have already found out something, Mr. Simpson, but unfortunately what we have found does not clarify anything and I still believe that it obscures it more.

We found an abandoned cart several days ago on the block of an inn in the Plaza de los Sauces and I asked him to accompany me to examine it to see if it was his companion's. But if it is, little else we can know.

"From what the innkeeper said, it was left there by a fellow in his sixties, of good stature, dark, with gray hair. He slept at the inn and the next morning, he got up early, left the inn and returned at lunchtime. He left, came back in the evening, and left again around half past nine, never to return.

The owner was waiting for the return of the owner of the vehicle, as he assumed that he was not going to leave it there in exchange for the day of lodging, since the cart is worth much more than the debit.

As he said, I was already beginning to be alarmed by the delay and was about to realize the fact. This is all.

"Did you say when it arrived?

On the 18th in the afternoon and on the 19th he disappeared.

"The address matches that of our colleague, but they must have taken the name.

"Indeed, but something strange has happened. The person in charge of scoring the entries had the inkwell turned over in the book and there are two completely illegible names. One is the owner of the vehicle.

"And you don't remember the name?

"He says no.

"Well, we can go examine the wagon.

They both went to the inn and as soon as Leslie raised the heavy hulk to his face, he exclaimed excitedly:

"It's Bird's, Mr. Sheriff... I know her very well.

"In that case, it only remains to find out what became of its owner. As I say, I have not the slightest news that any body was found in those days without identifying or identifying that name. We have to admit that if he was murdered, he was taken away from here and hidden in some accident on the ground. I will have to order the exploration of the suitable places to hide a corpse.

"Haven't you found out anything about that Adam's owl?

"It is still early, but without personal signs it is not so easy. By the name alone, he had to be well known here for some signs of him to be given.

"I take care of the difficulty and I regret that I cannot do something to help you.

"What my men cannot accomplish, you will not accomplish.

"Presumably. It only remains for me to stand idly by and wait. The unfortunate thing is that, given the distance and the lack of communications, it is impossible for me to send any message to my colleagues, informing them of what is happening. If it takes too long to find out something practical, I will be forced to return to the village and report what is happening, even if I have to return later. If it took too long, they would also end up fearing for my life and I have left relatives there who would be distressed by my fate.

"We will try to hurry as much as possible. I've already traded my partner in Sterling to track down Swan and force him to come here quickly. Perhaps from what that man declares, some new ray of light may emerge.

Leslie, hopeless and sadder and sadder, thinking of the tragic fate Bird might have suffered, retired to the inn. He was not in the mood to visit the village, least of all the warehouses in search of something to bring to his fiancée. Things were not enough to think about superfluous expenses, when they were threatened with imminent ruin.

And thinking about this, his anger was infinite.

As a good settler, he loved Mother Earth as he could love his own life. He had always lived by the effort of cultivating it; the land had offered him his daily sustenance to a greater or lesser degree and he could not renounce that piece of land scratched with sweat and that promised all the well-being and happiness he had dreamed of when he managed to marry Margaret.

Do not! He couldn't give her up and he wouldn't give up. Neither Greene, nor Swan, nor anyone else would tear from him, that land that was the basis of his existence, because he would defend him by shooting against whoever it was, under the protection of the law or against it, because the legality that Swan could invoke would be a usurped legality.

Weakened, he sat down in one of the many old wicker chairs in the hall. Next to the chair was a wide table and, scattered on it, some outdated newspapers and a couple of battered magazines from the East.

Mechanically, without knowing what he was doing, he picked up a magazine, but put it down right away. Then, he rummaged through several widely read newspapers, and when he was about to leave the last one because he lacked the courage to read things that did not interest him, his eyes stumbled upon an epigraph of an event that was related in it.

The release was headed by a headline that read:

MYSTERIOUS CRIME

Without knowing why, he was intrigued by the title and began to read avidly. When he learned that the wounded man had been found in an alley near the Plaza de los Sauces, his heart beat violently since the inn where Bird had stayed was located in that square.

And when he finished reading the story, there was no doubt that the seriously injured man who had been taken to the hospital in an agonizing state was Bird.

And perhaps this explained the sheriff's assertion, by assuring that no unidentified body had been found. He hadn't found, because Bird had been picked up alive and taken to the hospital. And now, what was missing for his suspicions to be confirmed, was to know if the wounded man had died, if he had been buried and if there was any more evidence that had just clarified his doubts.

Hastily, he picked up the newspaper and reported to the sheriff's offices.

The latter, observing him pale and nervous, asked:

"What's wrong with you, Mr. Simpson?

"I dont know. I think I have discovered a clue to locate my missing partner, but I preferred to come and see him so that he may be the one with his authority to carry out the pertinent investigation, if you do not know something more specific about this.

And he handed him the newspaper, saying:

See the date. The newspaper is from the 20th and Bird disappeared on the 19th at half past nine. On the other hand, he was staying at the Posada de los sauces and the body of the dying man was discovered in an alley near the square. This seems to claim that it is Bird and that he was murdered while returning to his lodge.

The sheriff, after reviewing the document, replied:

"It is very possible that he is right. The wounded man was found at dawn and at the hospital they told me that they did not give a penny for his life. They agreed to notify me if he died or recovered and I could testify, but so far, they have not provided me with any news of him. The truth is that he had forgotten this event and I have not linked it to the disappearance of his partner. But we can remedy this immediately by going to the hospital to see the wounded man.

"Couldn't he have died and ...?

"I don't think so, because had I died they would have given me the corresponding part.

"But they haven't called him to take a statement either.

"True, but this may indicate that, against the doctors' prognosis, he has not died, although his recovery, given the seriousness he presented, has not yet been achieved and the wounded man lives, but is still unable to speak.

"We will visit him and if he is who we suppose, the case will be clarified. I trust that, if he has not died, after so many days, it is that the doctors are achieving the miracle of preserving his life and that at some point science will triumph in this fight against death. Come with me, then, although the time is a little late, for me all hours are good and no one will deny me entry and examination of the wounded man.

With her soul on a thread, Leslie accompanied the sheriff. He was mentally asking God that that incognito injured was Bird and that he continue to preserve his life, not because of what he could clarify about the event, but because he deserved to continue living.

When they arrived at the hospital, the doctor who stood guard greeted them asking:

"What brings you here at this hour, Sheriff?

"I come to know what happened to a very seriously injured man who was found several days ago in an alley near the Plaza de Los Sauces and of which you have not given me the slightest news.

"Indeed, Sheriff, but no case has yet been made to notify you.

"The wounded man has been a week closer to the grave than to life, but miraculously death has been avoided, since the stab he received in the back interested him in the lung and some other organ, which made us fear a fatal outcome.

But fortunately, within gravity, it seems that the danger is subsiding without this meaning that it does not yet exist. The wounded man is strong as a buffalo and he recovers slowly; however, he has not yet regained consciousness, nor do we know when he will be able to.

"If it continues like this, it is possible that in a few days he will begin to realize that he is still in the world and may say something, but until now it is a body that breathes calmly and nothing else.

"For this reason, we have not been able to notify him. He is neither deceased nor in a position to declare anything.

"Well, at least the news is kind of nice, since apparently that poor man is saving himself from falling into the grave.

"Yes, and I suppose that when he visits us at this time, it is because he brings him something related to the wounded man.

"Indeed, this man who accompanies me suspects that it is a colleague of his who came here to carry out some formalities and who they have not heard from since he said goodbye to him. We came to take a look at it to see if it's the same.

"Very good. In that case, follow me.

He took them to a small room where only the wounded man was. It did not suit him that there was noise around him, and for this reason he had been isolated from others. Leslie took a quick glance at the patient's shrunken, bearded, pale face to recognize him.

"It's the same, Sheriff" he stated in a voice veiled by emotion. This is our colleague Victor Bird.

"I was almost certain of it," replied the sheriff, "and I believe that this identification completes the story.

The doctor asked:

"Have they managed to find out who the savage was who stabbed him?

"Yes, we know the name and we know the motive, what we do not know is who the criminal is and what his whereabouts are, but we will try to locate him.

And now, it only remains for me to thank you for the interest that you have all put in saving the life of this unhappy man and to reiterate my request that as soon as he is in a position to speak, you let me know.

"Don't worry, that is how it will be done.

They both shook the doctor's hand and left the hospital.

On the street, Leslie commented:

"Now I am infinitely happy to have embarked on the adventure of making this annoying trip. I cannot abandon this man; and I will do everything in my power to take care of him as soon as he is able to return to the village.

"But I fear that this will go on for a long time and will force me to make a new trip. I can't have a hundred men uncertain, not just about what has happened to Bird, but what may have happened to me, if it takes me too long to return.

"If you can wait a couple of days or three, maybe in that time we'll be able to find out something. I await a reply from Sterling for the buyer of that record to appear, to see what he tells us; and regarding the so-called Adam Greene, I will issue orders throughout the district so that the sheriffs are attentive, in case at any time he makes an appearance somewhere where he can be located.

For now, I admit your complaint and accuse you of attempted murder and robbery. When he shows up, I hope he doesn't have a great time.

"Two or three days, and even four or five, I can wait. My colleagues know or suspect that the mission that I bring can be laborious, and during that time, they will not feel very nervous. I don't want to leave here without being able to talk to Bird and know when the least he's out of the woods.

"If he continues to recover as the doctor has indicated, it is possible that by that time he will be in a position to make a statement. It would be very interesting to complement the information with what you say.

So arm yourself with patience and hold your nerves. For now, your partner's life seems to be safe, and that is already an asset in your favor. We will see if we can get other positives that allow us to annul that damn record and give them back their lands and the tranquility that they are losing.

"I wish! Be that way, Sheriff, because otherwise I'm afraid that there by the river, very unpleasant things are going to happen to each other.

They said goodbye and Leslie prepared to wait for further events if they occurred.

He had reassured himself of Bird's fate; but the very serious problem of ownership of his lands remained, and this one did overwhelm him.

The next day was a blank day. Impatient, he made a visit to the hospital, where he was told that Victor was still more or less, but slowly improving.

And the next day he received a notice from the sheriff to urgently report to their offices.

Hoping that the sheriff had managed to find out something about Adam, a tall, flexible, dark, determined-looking, relatively elegantly dressed fellow quickly showed up at the offices where the sheriff was meeting.

The sheriff made the introduction of the stranger, saying:

"He introduced you to Mr. Ludwing Swan, who has just arrived from Sterling on my order of presentation. This man is Leslie Simpson, one of the settlers settled in Abilene.

"Nice to meet you" said Swan, smiling, as he offered his hand to the settler.

He shook it softly, without any effusion, despite understanding that the trafficker was not guilty of the annoying situation that beset him.

"Well, Mr. Swan, since it was interesting that Mr. Simpson was present at our interview, since he is an interested party in it, I have delayed our talking at length about the reason for your call. Now we can do it, without having to repeat the conversation again.

"From what I have been able to verify in the registry, you have registered in your name a certain piece of land nestled on the banks of Smoky Hill, where a hundred settlers have founded a town called Abilene, have you not?

"Justly.

"And you were sold by a guy named Adam Greene, right?

"This is stated in the registry.

"How did Adam offer you that bargain?

"Because he needed money, he said.

"Do you know Adam from anything other than that operation?

"Well ... how to meet him, I did know him, but not much. I have seen him a few times here in the gambling dens, but our treatment was not one of friendship. One known as many.

"What reason was there for me to offer you that sale?

"Perhaps knowing that I was looking for a place that would not cost me dearly, to build a small ranch and be able to house the cattle with which I traffic. Sometimes it is not easy to buy a tip of cattle and sell it at the same time and that created a problem for me to place the cattle while I was able to sell it.

And did he know? Had you told him?

"Do not. He had spoken several times in those places of the need he had to find that land and he must have heard it. That's why he offered it to me.

"Did you know where that property came from?

"Me? Why did he have to know?

"It is always interesting to know the origin of what one buys, especially when it is offered so generously, since you will have calibrated that a town with a hundred plots of land in operation and a meadow to found a ranch, are worth much more than that. minimum figure of ten thousand dollars that he gave for her.

"When you are in pressure of money, many things are sold for less value, sometimes cattle at a lower price than you pay for them and if you are a man you felt a need for money, it is justified.

"Just a moment. Wasn't it shocked that a property that had been registered a week earlier was offered so urgently and at such a low price?

"I didn't have to meddle in the seller's private business. This one had the registration of that land in order, I bought it from a notary as it is accredited and I proceeded to register it in my name. Everything that concerns who sold it to me, is something that does not affect me.

"Possibly, yes, Mr. Swan, because that land was registered in the name of Adam Greene, through an assassination attempt and the theft of all the documentation that the victim carried to verify the registry in the name of the 100 settlers established there.

"And he must think that it may affect him, because if Greene is arrested and he confesses as it must, that, in effect, he tried to assassinate the bearer of the plans and stole them to search the land in his name, the authority legal will have to consider the fact and it would surely annul the primitive record, which would be stripped of that purchase that, if it seemed like a good deal, it would be turned into a very bad one.

Swan revolted when he heard the sheriff.

"Hey, I don't know the origin of that registration, nor do I care, what I do know is that I bought it, paid for it and duly registered it. The land is mine and ...

"Don't be upset, because you won't be able to upset things. The Law reaches everyone to a greater or lesser degree and when someone steals an object and sells it, both are covered by the same code. The one who stole to a greater degree and the one who bought, if he did so in good faith, will not suffer the rigors of a criminal sanction, but will lose what he paid for the object, since it has a defined owner and he did not sell it, but that it was stolen, but if the acquisition was made knowing the origin of the object, then the code reaches both.

"This should be put into his head so that he is not misled if things go where they should go and the land is returned to its true owners.

And was I going to lose that ten thousand dollars?

"You can proceed against the one who cheated you by selling you what was not yours and getting double prosecuted. If you are creditworthy, you would get what you wrongly paid back.

"Is a guy who sells ten worth for one solvent?

"I guess not, but ... loyally I would not buy blindly if they offered it to me, a brilliant valued at a thousand dollars, percent, because it is always possible to suspect that the origin is not very clear.

"There was a legal record that guaranteed it.

"A legal registration to a certain extent, One is the owner of a thing, as long as the contrary is not proven.

And am I the one who has to lose out?

"He is exposed to it, as soon as there is reliable evidence that shows the theft. When this happens, you may lose ten thousand dollars, but someone will lose their life at the same time.

"The life of that buharro matters little to me, what matters to me is my money.

"I am not selfish and I am willing for those settlers and I to reach an agreement, if, as you say, the land was going to be registered in their name. Both of us have been scammed and it is fair that we all suffer losses a little.

"If they are willing, I will not demand anything more from them than what I have paid for the land. That they all pay me for the ownership of their parcels those ten thousand dollars that I have paid, which is not much divided between a hundred and that they leave the piece of meadow free to build the ranch and keep my cattle. I think I am right.

But Leslie, intervening, replied:

"That thing that you put in fantasy reason, because being we the true owners of the land we would have to lose the ten thousand dollars in your favor and you, instead of losing, would win that piece of prairie equivalent to the same amount of land that we occupy together.

"Of course I lose. I could sell that for four or five times what I paid for.

"He would lose it if the purchase had been legal, but not being it, that belief is frustrated to the point of warning him not to try to sell it quickly to get rid of that burden, because he will not succeed. The registry has an order to immobilize the ownership of that land until it is clarified in some way who can or should be the true owner.

"And how is it going to be clarified and when?

"When Adam is caught and he declares what he has to declare. Only then can the judges have the last word.

"What if that man didn't look or ... turn up dead?

"Why should he appear dead?

"It is an assumption, especially since he is a man with an equivocal life, who frequents gambling dens, drinks, plays hard and fights. One day, someone can put two ounces of lead in his body and then ...

"The sky can also sink over us, or an earthquake can occur that annihilates us all. I can't go that far as long as reality doesn't take me there.

"Good, but since we have to stick to the moment, the moment is one and it is clear. As long as the contrary is not proven, I am the owner of that land and I can dispose of it as owner and lord.

"Until a certain point. You cannot try to sell it, because the sale would not be accepted in the Registry and because the settlers are not willing to buy it, because it is yours.

"But I have the right to expel them from there if they refuse to make an arrangement and rent it to whoever pays the rent just enough.

"I hope he resigns himself and doesn't try. He would meet the hostility of a hundred desperate men and I don't think he is in a position to impose himself on them by force.

The smuggler's anger grew every time the sheriff confronted him with arguments that nullified his views.

And beside himself, he bellowed:

"What can happen is my thing. I am the legal owner of that land and I will do what I see fit, as long as there is nothing greater than my strength and right that prevents it. If the culprit is that pig Adam, find him, save him, but leave me alone.

"We will look for you and hang you if possible, but with this you will not gain anything, because if you are tried and hanged for crime and robbery, the judges will annul the registration and order to put it in the name of the settlers. Don't forget this so you don't get your hopes up.

Thank you for such a healthy warning. I repeat that as long as the situation does not change and if it does I am the legal owner of those lands and as such I will proceed. The obstacles that they intend to oppose me, I'll see how I eliminate them. And if you have nothing more to say to me, I will withdraw.

"Nothing, unless you look at what you are doing, for now you will not act with your eyes closed.

Swan stormed out of the office, leaving the sheriff and Leslie behind.

CHAPTER VII

BIRD MAKES DECLARATION

After a moment of silence, Leslie commented:

"I don't like this man at all, Sheriff.

"And me neither.

"Do you have any antecedents of him?

"None, but I can ask for it.

"I think you would do well to do it. I do not know why I am convinced that he has blatantly lied to us about some things.

"In which ones?

"One, in denying that I know that Adam anything more intimately than in meeting him in some gambling dens. I am sure you know him well and may even know where he is. You don't buy things from a stranger, just like that, without inquiring about them.

"So, you think he knows that the search was made on the basis of a robbery ...

"If you don't know, you must have suspected. Perhaps he was unaware that the robbery was the result of an assassination attempt, which makes things more serious.

"And proof that he does not feel safe, is that cable that he extended to us so that we could buy the plots for the money he has paid, leaving the prairie for him ... If he had not had that fear, he would not have made the proposal the first time. exchange.

"I also suspect that and something else. Sometimes, having the tongue is very helpful, because certain phrases can be interpreted in many ways and at some point constitute a noose woven by one of one's own.

"What do you mean?

"To the question she asked by putting a lot of interest in her about what would happen if Adam turned up dead without time to confess his crime.

"It's true; I had not fallen in that.

"That is why I say that sometimes, it is better to think one thing, but weigh its importance before saying it. He has tried to justify it by alluding to the fact that that buharro could die the victim of a fight and a fight prepares with advantage to win the action and get rid of it.

"It's true and if he knows Adam well and knows where to find him, there would be nothing to recriminate him for the sale he made, but he could consolidate it forever, if he got rid of Adam before you could get hold of him. Then, the theft could not be proven and the record would be firm forever.

"It's just what I was thinking and this forces me to take tough measures with that guy. I'm going to get very specific reports on him from the Sterling Sheriff and I'm going to try to put someone behind him to watch him just in case. If what I think is true and he has devised to get rid of the seller to cut short any possibility of having the property of those lands seized from him, he himself will lead us to the man we are looking for and who knows if even by settling a conflict, it will be created another more dangerous for him.

"So, as long as the Sterling Sheriff sends me the reports that he has or can collect, I am going to send one of my commissioners to the town with an order to stick to the shadow of that man, to see if he will lead him to the most we are interested in catching.

"Do you think that will be possible?

"I don't know, but something has to be done to achieve it.

"I say it, because I am thinking of something that can be wise.

"Talk up, you have come up with some useful things ... why can't you think of others?

"Thank you for the good concept you have of me. I was referring to this worthy of being taken into account. Adam knows that he has deceived Swan, or at least that he can put him in a bad situation, so bad, that he forces him to report him. I think I can assure you that that Swan after his crime, will have been aware of the fate that his victim may have suffered, since only by totally killing him can he live calmly and therefore, it must be certain that he will have been pending to know what happened with Bird.

"This, only the press has been able to tell her and it is not an illusion to say that she has been aware of her, and that she will have read how my partner was picked up dying and taken to hospital. Not knowing that he has died, he will be forced to hide, in case Bird has been able to testify by denouncing him and because then, Swan would know he was deceived and can look for him to ask him to account for what he has done with him. If possible, I would ask you a favor.

"Which one?

"Let him publish in the press here, a very visible release, in which it is announced that the dying man who was found in the Callejón de los Sauces, has died after many days of being unconscious, without being able to declare or identify his person. This, which can be read by Adam, would reassure him to the point of abandoning the darkness and showing himself again in the light. sure that no one could accuse him of the crime and theft, and even Swan himself would have nothing to reproach him for, since the purchase would be insured.

It may be that my idea is useless, but it could also be that it was a good bait to force him to bite into it. Since it hurts no one to publish the news like this, if it works, it would help us locate that guy, since, believing himself free from all danger, he would not hesitate to show himself in public as if he had done nothing.

The sheriff, after pondering the suggestion, said:

"I think he's right. All that can happen is that it is useless, but nothing is lost by trying. Today I will speak with the director of the newspaper here, I will explain what I want and ask him to publish the news. I am sure that he will do so, because if it works, it would be a good report for him at a more or less distant date.

"Thank you, and since I don't think more can be done at the moment, I will leave you, although I will come to visit you to see what new news you can provide.

"I intend to stay four or five more days, to see if in that time something arises that clarifies the situation and if it does not, I will return to the town to report to my companions, but with the firm intention of returning here again and not move until everything is solved or we lose hope of getting it.

My trip will serve to put my companions on guard so that they will not be surprised by Swan if he shows up there and tries to convince them to buy his plots, even at a low price. They could not at the moment, because we do not have money and our crops are stored without selling yet, but perhaps he was looking for some trick to hunt them down.

And if it is presented with people willing to impose themselves by the brave, they are prepared to respond in the same tone.

"Agree. I'm going to the newspaper now and file my report so my commissioner can take it to Sterling and deliver it to the sheriff. I hope that on the ground they will achieve something more than at a distance.

Leslie said goodbye to the sheriff with a strong handshake and returned to the inn.

Now he did not feel as pessimistic as before. Bird's status seemed promising and everything that was discovered seemed to be a solid pedestal to base on future actions, which would lead them to the success they longed for. What made him bitter the most was being away from Margaret and thinking about the anguish that she could be suffering from ignoring her whereabouts and what might happen to her, but events demanded it and he could not go back from the management that had begun.

The next day, as the sheriff had promised, the local newspaper published in a conspicuous place and in striking characters, the news of Bird's death. It was emphasized in the text that he had not been able to make any statement so it was unknown who he was and who could have killed him.

That was the bait laid out to see if someone would bite.

Adam was the fish they hoped to catch on the false hook, since if he read the loose, he would consider himself completely safe and without any liability whatsoever.

The sheriff's commissioner went out to fulfill his mission and the first reports regarding Swan's personality arrived the next day.

According to the sheriff, he was listed as a cattle dealer, but there were doubts about his honesty as a dealer. His businesses were carried out outside the town, so the sheriff did not know how to operate, but stressed that on one occasion he was intervened by a tip of stolen cattle. He had covered himself by showing a receipt, which listed a rancher as the seller, although it was later found that the receipt had been falsified.

Swan had escaped serious disgust, claiming that he had acquired the cattle in good faith, believing that the sale was made by the team foreman, who had given him the receipt. The false foreman could not be located and the matter was left dead.

Swan had a team of half a dozen men who took care of driving the cattle, but none of them was from the village, so there was nothing he could say about that team.

This just increased the sheriff's misgivings about the dealer. He was increasingly convinced that he had bought the land knowing that the sale was not legal, although he had not suspected that the matter was in such a messy and dangerous state.

Two days later, he received a new report. Swan had left the village together with two other men who were supposed to be members of his team, but the direction he had taken was unknown.

Since the sheriff had ordered his sheriff to follow him, he was confident that he would not lose his track and could send him some more useful report.

For four more days, the situation did not change and Leslie, already nervous, wanting to see himself in his fields, even if it was only for a couple of days, visited the sheriff to communicate his intention to leave, but with the idea of returning as soon as he informed his companions of everything that happened.

"I'm leaving tomorrow morning," he said, "but before leaving I would like to pay Bird a visit to see how he is and I trust that, if he regains consciousness in my absence, you will take care of him and tell him everything. what have we done. Warn him that I must return in ten or twelve days and that I will stay here until he is well and can begin the journey to Abilene.

"Don't worry, I will make sure that you are well informed and well cared for.

When they visited the hospital in the middle of the afternoon, Leslie was pleasantly surprised. According to the doctor, the patient had begun to show signs of life that morning and twice he was vaguely aware of his surroundings. The doctor was confident that if he continued like this he might be able to give a statement the next day, albeit of a short duration.

This forced Leslie to delay his departure one more day. If Bird spoke, the next day he could leave fully informed of what had happened.

And with devouring impatience, he let the hours of the next day pass, until late afternoon when he and the sheriff returned to the hospital.

Again the doctor attending Bird greeted them saying:

"He has reacted quite well and coordinates his words. He has asked me several questions which I have refused to answer, so as not to tire him. I told you that tonight I would give you permission to speak, but very little.

He led them to the room where the wounded man was. He was looking better, for someone had shaved off the tangled beard that covered his face. He had grown thin and his eyes were very bright, but he showed the mettle of his rock-hard humanity.

Sensing footsteps in the room, he turned his head and recognizing his fellow exile, he muttered:

"Leslie! ... You ... here ...!

He approached, took her sweaty hand and with an accent that wanted to be firm but was trembling, said:

"Listen to me, Bird, yes, it is me and I am here as you will see, but I am going to ask you one thing. The doctor authorized us to see him and talk to him, since it is essential that we know something about what has happened to him, but before he tells us, he will have to listen to me to tell him how I am here and what has happened since you fell wounded until now. My story will save you from asking tiresome questions and will only limit you to giving us an account of what happened. Therefore, listen to me and do not speak.

Leslie gave him a detailed account of his entire odyssey since he decided to leave the town to go to Hitchinson to find out what had happened to him, and then all the steps taken up to that moment.

The rude former caravanner made tremendous efforts to speak and to suppress the anger that dominated him and on two occasions when he tried to speak, the doctor who attended him cut off his gesture saying:

"Don't speak yet, or you'll force me to send these gentlemen out of here. His state does not yet allow certain freedoms.

When Leslie finished his story, the old man hoarsely:

"Thank you Leslie, you are very good and I will never pay ...

"Stop using useless words and tell what happened, but in the most concise way possible.

Bird recounted how she had found Adam and how they had greeted each other after years of not seeing each other. He angrily confessed that perhaps because of having drank a couple of whiskeys with Adam, his tongue had spoken more than necessary and how that night, after having dinner together as they crossed the alley on the way to the inn, he had felt hurt and lost consciousness. without later knowing anything else.

Only when he regained consciousness had his imagination worked to search for the reason for this unexpected attack and had he suspected the truth. Adam tried to assassinate him to steal all the papers and search the land in the name of another.

The sheriff forced him to be silent, saying:

"Well, don't talk anymore and just answer a few questions. Adam told you that he worked for a cattle dealer, didn't he say the dealer's name?

"He didn't say it, nor was it interested to me:

"Well, I'm suspecting that he worked for Swan and was part of his team. This is clearing up some dark spots and Swan is going to be very compromised to get out of the trance with flying colors.

"I am now convinced that he worked for that guy and that his activities were not very legal. Therefore, because he worked for him, he offered to sell the registry, knowing that he was exposing himself to many serious things if he tried to exploit the proceeds of the theft.

"We will again reach out to Swan to force him to loosen his tongue. He has to know a lot about Adam and he has to tell us.

"At the moment, you do not have to worry or torment yourself thinking about what happened. We hope to clarify things so that this record is annulled and becomes your property as is right.

Bird took the sheriff's hand and muttered:

"Get it for what you want most, Sheriff, because if you don't get it and my colleagues lose their land because of my stupidity, this life that the doctors have insisted on sticking to my body, would be of no use to me and I myself I would rip it off as punishment for my mistake.

"Don't be pessimistic and calm down. I repeat that things are on the right track and that sooner or later everything will be solved.

"So be it, Bird" stated Leslie. And don't do stupid things. I am leaving tomorrow to inform my colleagues about what is happening, but as soon as they are informed, I will return, you will not be able to leave here for fifteen or twenty days and we trust that by then everything will have been solved and you will return with me without worries.

"May God so please, and not for me, but for you.

Leslie and the sheriff said goodbye to the wounded man, and on the street, the second said:

"I believe that, indeed, you should return to your lands and leave this in my hands. Swan is well tied and I will take care to tie him better. Everything will be pending that Adam is located and I will move heaven and earth so that they can find him somewhere.

Leslie thanked him for the interest he was putting in this matter and prepared to leave the next day. He was looking forward to getting there to come back again and not to lose track of that pair of rascals who had set out to ruin them.

CHAPTER VIII

ONE FAILED ATTEMPT

In Abilene, concern was still reigning and not because of Leslie whose return was not yet expected, but because of what might have happened to Bird and because of the unknown involved in not knowing if their lands had been duly registered or not.

Up to five horsemen, who stopped in it contemplating the panorama and making signs with their hands as if they were planning to settle a new colonist in it.

The third member of the committee appointed to settle any issues that might arise between them was alarmed and as he was also a tough and violent man, he decided to go out to meet the newcomers, to ask them what they were doing there and what they were up to.

The quintet consisted of Swan himself and four of his team's pawns. The dealer had made up his mind not to give up, and, disdaining the sheriff's warnings, set out to take possession of the land and probe the settlers' spirits.

He tried to intimidate them and later, to temporize and tear leases from them when they were convinced that they had lost the right to consider this as theirs. He had to maneuver quickly before Leslie returned, knowing she was still in the village when he left it.

The settler named Martyn Dickson, came forward and after greeting them coldly, asked:

"Will you please tell me what you are doing here?

"Why not? "Asked Swan smiling." We are studying the terrain to decide where we are going to build my ranch.

"I am afraid that you have made a mistake, gentlemen. This is not free ground, but quite the opposite. It belongs to our community of settlers and the ranch that will soon be built here will be our property.

"I'm afraid you are wrong, sir," replied Swan coldly. This land and all that you own is my property. I bought it three weeks ago from its rightful owner, according to Hutchinson's land registry, and it's mine. If you have any doubts, I bring with me the documents that certify me as the absolute owner of all this and although I intend to establish a ranch here for my cattle, I do not intend to drive them out of here, if they agree to us agreeing by signing lease agreements. I like to live in peace with people, but I also like to get the proper product out of my property.

The settler, who had listened to him with his mouth open and a strange trembling throughout his body, stammered:

"What... what... does it say? What ... is this yours?

"I have said that and I bring the documentation that proves it. I bought it from whoever had it duly registered in their name and I can show you the papers so that there is no doubt.

The settler was stunned for a moment. His first suspicion was that Bird had betrayed them, registering everything in his name, to sell it and escape with the proceeds of the looting. This justified that they had not heard from him again and that, instead of suffering an accident, what he had done was something unspeakable.

But refusing to admit it, he exclaimed:

"What does it say? Which Victor Bird has registered this in your name and then sold it to you?

"Victor Bird? I don't know who that man is. The record was verified by a certain Adam Greene, who has been the one who transferred it to me.

Martyn breathed with some relief, when realizing that his companion had not been a traitor, and with energy, he replied:

"Excuse me for saying that we do not admit that this is your property. The record must have been verified by our colleague Bird, who was the one who left here with the precise documentation and there must be a misunderstanding on your part.

"For my part there is no misunderstanding, sir, here is the register and the designated place. Everything that is part of this small valley, including the parcels and the town called Abilene, is included in the record sheet. You can check it yourself.

And taking a folder with various papers out of his pocket, he handed it over saying:

"See them and then tell me if you think there is confusion.

The settler, without leaving his astonishment, took the papers and examined them. There would be no confusion, since there was a small plan and the boundaries of the plots.

Returning the folder, he replied:

"You will be right, sir, but I think you have been ripped off. This is very ours and we are not willing to allow anyone to come and take it from us after we have sweated blood on these abandoned lands.

"It will be as it says, but in two years they have had time to register them. If someone knew about such abandonment and registered them in their name, it is your fault. I only know that I have acquired it legally, as this record shows and the rest does not matter to me.

"I offer you the possibility of reaching a beneficial agreement without looking back, but abiding by the present, if you reject it, worse for you because then you will force me to appeal to other less friendly means to defend what is mine.

"We will also appeal to those media to defend what is more ours than theirs, even if they think otherwise.

"Are you challenging me? Swan asked aggressively.

"You challenge us that it is not the same. Here we nailed our heels two years ago and here they will remain nailed as long as we have the courage to defend it. Only with our feet forward can they get us out of those fields.

"And this is my opinion, I can tell you that it will be that of the rest of my teammates. I will give you an account of his claim, but I suspect that he has very little chance of settling on this land a single cattle, not a single log to build that ranch.

"We'll see that. I have the legal force for it.

"We have another more expeditious force.

"Do you think I can't have it?

"I do not know, but that will be seen in due course. Therefore, if you want to avoid uselessly spilling blood, get out of here and there will be no fight.

"I also know how to keep my heels on the ground when I decide to nail them hard.

"Well ... there you with the consequences.

And turning around, he walked away from the fields, to inform his companions of Swan's claims.

He was furious at the energetic and aggressive attitude of the settler. If his companions took the same bad attitude, he could carry out his bravado of not abandoning this, when with that small handful of men he could not face a hundred enraged settlers.

Martyn was quick to spread the word so that everyone would immediately gather in the town square. The meeting was of an urgent nature and not a single minute could be lost.

Margaret, understanding herself, ran in search of Martyn asking:

"What is happening? What do these men want?

The settler gave her a brief account of the case, while the settlers were coming and the young woman tense, exclaimed:

"How could that be, Martyn? If our lands have been registered in the name of another, it must be admitted that it was because Bird was killed and his papers stolen. Bird was a man of integrity, incapable of committing such a betrayal.

"That's what I think, but be that as it may, the lands have been registered in someone else's name and sold to that guy. It must have been so, Margaret.

"But ... how has Leslie not found out about that and has already come to find out so that we know what happened?

"I do not know, but ... you have to trust that he will not be idle and that he will be working to clarify the case. Leslie is quite a man and will know how to proceed according to the circumstances.

"I have always believed it that way, but ... if nothing can be done to avoid this dispossession, what can we do to defend what is our life?

"There is only one way; defend it with weapons in hand.

"Yes, but against the law, although this law is not the legal one.

"We will expose ourselves. Between dying abandoned in the meadow, or with weapons in hand, the latter is preferable.

"That man will appeal to the authorities. They protect you.

"The Law is a long way from here and not one sheriff or two would accomplish anything. I doubt he can get a squad of cavalry sent to shoot us out of here.

It is unfortunate what happens, but we must arm ourselves with courage and face all plunder. Before long, Leslie will return and he will inform us fully and tell us what to do.

"Do you think... that... will return? She asked, distraught.

Why shouldn't he?

"What if ... they have set a trap for him, how could they have set it for Bird?

"Leslie was forewarned and is not a confident old man like Bird, but an overly clever man. I have no fears about his life.

"May God hear you is what I ask of you.

Martyn separated from the young woman to rejoin the rest of the settlers in the plaza. They had all guessed that something serious was happening, when they had been summoned so urgently.

Martyn briefly informed them of the reason for the presence of these men in the prairie and of the rights he claimed to own their lands.

The uproar that the product news was huge. They all raised their arms to the sky with clenched fists and swore that only lifeless would they be ripped from there. When the settler finished explaining what was happening, someone asked:

"How could that happen? What is Leslie doing that is not already here to inform us?

"When he has not come, his reasons will have. Our mission is not to understand the claims of these people and wait for their return to learn many things that we ignore, but what is urgent is not to allow these people to take possession of the prairie, I propose that you take your weapons and all of us together let us present there to invite them to disappear.

What if they refuse?

"Then, worse for them; We will shoot them.

No one refused to follow Martyn's directions and, requiring their weapons, they left the village to head for the prairie.

When Swan noticed the determined attitude of the settlers, he felt a chill of fear. A hundred armed men were too many men to deal with, especially when they were under the influence of surprise and rage.

"Watch out! "He warned." Let no one get nervous and shoot if they don't try. Let me speak.

The group of settlers advanced, brandishing revolvers or rifles. They were alert in case they were taken in by shots. When the compact group found themselves twenty paces from Swan, who had advanced a little with his pawns behind him, these also with cocked revolvers, he shouted:

"Don't be crazy and put down those weapons! Force is not the reason and at any moment they can suffer the consequences of letting their nerves jump.

"I have come in peace and with the desire to reach an agreement with you. It is not by shooting how certain things are fixed.

Martyn indifferently replied:

"He has already explained his reasons to us and I have explained ours. There is only one solution; Either they leave these lands within five minutes, or we will shoot them down and give them no new chance to return.

"Do you think you advance something with that? I can go back to the authorities to force them to vacate their plots and if they force me to do so, then there will be no settlement. I will be cruel and not allow a single one to settle. I think it is better to agree than to fight.

But Martyn energetically replied:

"There is no pact that is worth. Either they leave or I order them to shoot. Make up your mind at once.

The moment was terribly tragic. The colonists seemed ready to carry out the order of the one who commanded them and all realized that it was suicidal folly to accept the fight.

But for Swan, this was a humiliation that he had a hard time accepting. First, for the moral part and second, because he feared that, if he was forced to be absent in the prairie, things could roll badly for him and if Adam was discovered, he would end up confessing certain things that would invalidate that disputed property record , causing him to lose the ten thousand dollars he had paid.

But for now, brute force was on the side of the colonists and nothing could against it.

Rabid replied:

"Okay, you have wanted it that way and it will be. One day not far away, I will come with the necessary force to impose my rights and that day they will realize how crazy they have been not accepting my proposals. When you have something that is not legally yours, sooner or later you are stripped of it.

"Half a minute has passed, sir. If he loses the other medium by wasting verbiage, he forces us to shoot. Think it over

I was thinking and Swan turning to his men said:

"Let's go, but let them think that we don't do it forever. You will hear from us soon.

The group tugged at their horses' bridles and turned their haunches, leaving the meadow.

The settlers had won the first skirmish, but this didn't mean much. They realized that they were facing the Law and that this was very dangerous if the trafficker appealed to all the resources that favored him, to conclude by throwing everyone from their plots by hook or by crook.

But they were stubborn and desperate. They defended mother earth, the one that was theirs, the one that they had watered with the sweat of their foreheads, and they could not yield without a fight the fruit of that tremendous effort made.

∗ ∗ ∗

A day later, Leslie, having completed the first part of her work in Hitchinson, returned to the village eager to arrive as soon as possible to inform her companions of the news that had arisen and to reassure them about her person.

She did it on horseback, as she had gone, for the wagon left her in town for when she could return and bring Bird still convalescing.

He was more than thirty miles from the town walking along a deserted road, when in the distance and riding in the opposite direction, he discovered a group of horsemen who seemed to be following the Hitchinson way.

The settler was startled by the discovery. This straight-line route to Abilene was not frequented, and the presence of the horsemen did not impress him.

Would they return from their village? Had they gone there with the intention of committing plunder? It could be a small band of robbers and, if so, it would not be convenient for him to be discovered, since the least that could happen was that they attacked him and stole his mount.

And if that happened, thirty miles on foot was a lot of miles to go at best.

He would find a place to hide and try to catch a glimpse of the riders.

He quickly turned to his left, seeking protection from some boulders that rose almost to the edge of the path. They were large enough to hide him and his horse.

But despite the speed with which he executed the maneuver, he could not prevent one of the horsemen from discovering him when he was hiding in a hurry.

The rider addressing Swan exclaimed:

"Boss, a horseman was coming over there and he has hidden behind that conglomerate of stones. Do you think it could be some lone robber trying to attack us by surprise?

"Have you noticed the horse? He asked suddenly.

"Yes, although not very well. It is purple in color and has a good height.

Swan smiled strangely. He had just thought of Leslie, whose horse he had seen at the gates of the sheriff's office and judging him a dangerous fellow, had concealed that he was returning to his lands to account to his companions of the measures taken by the sheriff, to invalidate his right to dispose of what was acquired with such bad arts.

And if he let him get there, then he could say goodbye to intimidating the settlers and falsely extract a more or less large part of the money that he had paid to Adam and that he was doomed to lose.

And he had to avoid it. Nobody knew (or at least he believed it) that at that time he was visiting the settlers; Therefore, if afterwards a false cut was made and this could be corroborated by their laborers, then it would leave the colonists in ignorance of what happened and could continue to threaten them.

He had to suppress Leslie. Later, when his corpse was found so far from Hitchinson, as in those still half-desolate lands, there was no nearby authority, let them find out who had killed him.

And turning to the one who had sounded the alarm, he said:

“He is not a robber, but for me he is something worse. I need to eliminate it if I want to enjoy peace of mind by settling in that meadow where we can hide the cattle with impunity; You are going to help me liquidate him. I have a hundred dollars for each one if we make it out.

"What is there to do?

“For now, keep walking slowly, as if we hadn't seen you.

When we get to the rocks, you two go ahead, passing them, while the three of us lag behind and when I whistle, some to his right and others to his left, we surround him and shoot at him. You must believe that we have not discovered you and when you realize your mistake, it will be late.

“But in anticipation of something unforeseen, put the brim of your hat well over your eyes, so that it is not easy for him to recognize us. You have to take care of all the details.

After taking the precautions imposed by the trafficker, they continued advancing, looking askance at the cliffs in case they discovered the colonist stalking them.

Leslie, after hiding between the rocks, hid her horse between two stone blocks and since she could not see the path from there, she decided to climb another block of stones, from whose height it would be possible to keep an eye on the mysterious group.

That inspiration was going to save his life without realizing it.

He reached the stones and hidden by one of them, he could, discreetly peeking out from one of their sides, follow the advance of the horsemen.

And when they were quite close, he did not stop observing that they were wearing the brims of their hats very low and even more that, as they continued advancing, they had pulled them to lower them to the limit.

And this put him more on guard. The detail, where no one walked to see them, made him understand that there was a powerful reason for that maneuver and the reason was that they had discovered him and wanted to pass by depriving him of being able to see their faces.

More despite such precaution, one of the five caught his attention. He couldn't see his face, but from his silhouette he thought he recognized the cunning Swan.

And since he knew she had disappeared from Sterling shortly before he set out on the return trip, it didn't take much effort to guess that the reason for his absence had been to show up at Abilene to coerce his companions and who he knew to force them to. sign some document that would compromise them, in exchange for certain false promises of easy leases.

His first impulse was to wait until they were within gun range to shoot the Machiavellian dealer, but he held back. It took a lot of luck to fight five and come out victorious. He would have to let them pass ignoring them and march quickly to the village, to find out what his enemy had come to do in it.

He was following them attentively with the gaze of an eagle and the colt in his hand, when suddenly, he saw how the first two twisted the course of their mounts trying to reach the rocks on their left side, while the others did on the right.

And he understood the maneuver. They had seen him hide and were trying to lock him in a circle of revolvers. And he did not hesitate for a single moment. His Colt searched for what he believed to be Swan and shot him. He missed the shot, missing him because one of his pawns had crossed in front of the dealer when he fired and the bullet had achieved a different target than the one proposed. The pawn, well hit, fell from the horse abruptly, while the rest, realizing that there was no room for surprise, rushed to fire against the height where Leslie had ambushed.

But for the besieged settler there was a dangerous difficulty, and that was that he could not attend to two fronts at the same time. After his surprise shot and the fall of the pawn, the other four had quickly separated their horses from the vicinity of the rocks and were firing at a distance on both sides. Leslie swayed back and forth trying to keep track of the two groups. An oversight could make it easier for some of them to approach and hunt him down, since the protection of the rock was not enough more than to offer him a frontal parapet.

The colonist defended himself from the siege with energy and sometimes by shooting to the left and others to the right, he seemed to command respect for the besiegers, who did not dare to get too close for fear of suffering the fate of their companion.

Leslie used up the charge of his revolver and was forced to waste the precious time involved in putting half a dozen rounds back into the barrel; the cunning Swan, who seemed to be waiting for that hiatus in defense, when Leslie stopped firing to reload the weapon, advanced with his horse looking for the weak point from which to attack him.

And it was at the precise moment that the colonist with the Colt in a position to continue firing as he peeked around the side where the dealer had advanced, emitted a high-pitched cry of pain and dropped the revolver that, detaching from his hand, fell bouncing with a metallic noise as it hit the boulders.

Swan had hit him on the right arm, and as a result of the contraction, he had lost the revolver. At that moment he was at the mercy of his enemies, who seemed ready to finish him off.

Swan, realizing his success, shouted:

"It's ours, guys! You lost the Colt!

The four of them were preparing to concentrate their fire on the unhappy settler, when suddenly two thunderous detonations, produced not by a Colt, but by a rifle, vibrated and the gallop of an approaching horse was caught.

Swan realized the danger they were in. Their revolvers could not compete in range with a weapon of that caliber, and whoever came to Leslie's aid could safely shoot them.

And furious, he bellowed:

"Gallop everyone, don't let him overtake us or we are dead men!

And the quartet, abandoning the siege, undertook an amazing gallop, being pursued by the rifle of the mysterious apparition, but luckily for them, the mobility of the horses prevented them from hitting any of them.

The rider hesitated a moment between continuing the hunt or stopping. He supposed they had been shooting at someone hidden among the rocks and he feared he had been hit.

CHAPTER IX

NARROWING THE FENCE

The one who appeared before approaching the rocks and in anticipation of being attacked if he was mistaken for one of the fugitives, shouted:

"Who's there? Get out whoever it is without fear. I'm one of the Hitchinson sheriff's deputies.

Leslie; Upon hearing him, he breathed with relief and peering out from behind the rock while trying to contain the blood that flowed from the wound, he replied:

"I'm coming, Commissioner ... Wait a bit.

He worked his way down until he reached the full part, appearing before the commissioner. This, recognizing him, exclaimed:

"How are you?

"You know me right? I'm the one who filed the trespassing complaint with your sheriff.

"Of course I know him, and I'm the one who singled out the sheriff so he wouldn't lose sight of Swan.

"So, I have not been deceived in assuming that one of those who made up the group was that ruffian.

"No, you are not fooled, but what is that? Have you been hurt?

"Yes, although I don't think it's important. They took advantage of the moment when I needed to reload the revolver to come up and fire at me. They did it with such luck that, when they wounded me in the arm, I lost the revolver and if you did not arrive so in time, they would have finished me.

"Why?

"Perhaps because I have been the one who has discovered all the falsehood and who has been most determined to prevent this looting from being carried out.

"Well, come over and see that wound.

He helped her remove her arm from the sleeve of her jacket and examined her carefully.

"It doesn't seem serious, as you say. A bite of the bullet more spectacular than disturbing. Do you have a handkerchief?

"I have two.

"We will tie the injured limb tightly, which is all we can do at the moment and I suppose it will be able to hold out well until we reach the village.

"I hope so too. What will you do?

"My duty was not to detach myself from that guy, but in case you needed immediate help, I have let you escape. He had to choose between the two.

And I appreciate it. And since it is no longer easy for him to continue hunting, I invite him to come with me to the village. There we will explain everything that happened and immediately that I heal, we will return to undertake the return to Hitchinson. Now we really can't stop and let things take on bigger flights.

The commissioner, after a moment's meditation, replied:

"I accept your invitation, more than anything because I have exhausted the supplies that I had in my travel bag and need to replenish them to return.

"In that case, let's not waste time and get on the road. I hope that the wound does not prevent me from galloping and while we do so you will explain to me what has happened.

They mounted their horses after picking up Leslie's revolver, but already in the saddle the commissioner said:

"Just a moment. We cannot forget that one of his attackers has died. I am going to search his clothes to try to identify him and then I will leave him half hidden in the rocks among the rocks.

He seized his revolvers and his horse. He would take it to the village and later to Hitchinson.

When he climbed back into the saddle, he stood beside Leslie and they set off.

"Are you very upset? "I ask.

"No, it hurts of course, but it can be endured. More than thinking about the pain, I would like you to tell me what has happened.

"Not long, I followed Swan at a distance, who was joined by four more men, between Sterling and Hitchinson, it was hard for me to be able to follow them to the village without being discovered. Already there, and hidden in the depression that closes the small valley, I could observe how one of his companions came out to meet them and was talking with Swan. I do not know what they would say, but I do know that his companion withdrew to return later accompanied by all the settlers who showed up armed to the teeth. There was a violent discussion, but the quintet, being threatened by so many weapons, decided to leave the meadow and return again.

I was following them at a long distance, when I caught the maneuver made to go around the crags and then the thunder of the weapons. I did not imagine it was you, but whoever you were was obliged to intervene and intervenes. I have arrived well on time, because if I neglected a few minutes I would not have been able to collect more than his body.

"That's right and I thank you infinitely for your intervention. I've been in danger, but it seems to me that that buharro has taken a serious slip that is going to cost him dearly. If I had denounced that he wanted to kill me, I would have achieved nothing because he lacked witnesses, but having intervened, you are an authority, things vary. We'll see what that guy does now.

"What I feel is that I have lost her track and who knows if it will be easy to find her. In any case, you are and will be a witness to my behavior when I tell my boss why I have not been able to carry out your instructions to the letter.

"Don't worry, your boss is a very understanding man and will pick up on the situation.

"Now when we get to the village, we will rest for a day or two and immediately hit the road again. Things are becoming clearer and I hope that, not taking long, they will be completely clarified.

Leslie and the commissioner had to spend the night in the meadow and as the wound on his arm bothered the former too much, the commissioner had to untie his handkerchiefs and look for a stream where he could wash the wound. Then she applied a herbal poultice to him and bandaged him again.

The next day in the afternoon, they arrived in Abilene and as someone had discovered them moving towards there, the word quickly spread and they all abandoned their tasks to go out to meet them.

The one who ran the most was Margaret, who upon discovering that Leslie had her arm tied with handkerchiefs and her clothes stained with blood, exclaimed in anguish:

"Leslie, for all the saints! What has happened to you?

He jumped off the horse and hugging her smiling, he replied:

"It was nothing, my dear; a fall from the horse that has hurt me.

"Don't lie, that blood is not from a fall. You ... you have been shot.

"Well, it was actually a graze from a bullet, but don't be alarmed it wasn't a big deal. There is something more important than my injury.

And facing his companions who formed a great circle, he exclaimed:

"This is one of the Hutchinson Sheriff's Deputies. I owe my life to him, because he appeared unexpectedly when a group of five men had me cornered in some rocks and disarmed for having lost the revolver.

Martyn came forward saying:

"Five men? So ... they can only be those who have been here two days ago, with the pretense of settling in the prairie, claiming that they are the true owners of everything we thought was ours. What do you know about that, Leslie?

"I know many things and, if I have returned, it has been to reassure you and tell you not to lose your calm or despair. The thing is a bit muddled at the moment, but everything begins to develop in our favor. As soon as I leave you well informed and with specific instructions on what to do, we will rest for a day and return to Hutchinson the commissioner and I.

"Do not! "Cried Margaret." You no longer expose your life again. If good or evil is for everyone, let others expose theirs as well.

"Bird exposed her and has been between life and death for more than two weeks, but fortunately she is improving and the danger seems to recede. At this time, without this meaning that I give myself to be worth more than anyone else, the mission that still remains to be solved can only be carried out by me, because I have been the one who has intervened more directly in this matter and who has exposed it. Listen carefully to what I have to tell you and you will realize that I must be the one to continue the efforts until the matter is solved.

As everyone was eager for the enigma that contained the registry of their lands to be deciphered, Leslie informed them in all kinds of details, from when he arrived in Hutchinson, until the commissioner had intervened saving his life when they were about to assassinate him.

An angry Martyn joked:

"What a shame not to have known all that before, because if they had, those five buharros would have stayed here forever!

"It doesn't matter," Leslie commented. Now, Swan will be hard-pressed to get around where he can be recognized. The commissioner's report accusing him of having tried to assassinate me places him outside the law and he will be very careful not to try to coerce us again. He himself, being stupid, has cut his wings and in no case could he continue to claim those rights, because he would have to show his face and he would denounce himself.

"Of course, this does not solve the conflict, because what we need is that this stolen registration be annulled, both for Greene and Swan and that the lands that are ours be awarded to us. That is what I have to go to Hutchinson again, and you have to understand it that way.

But Margaret was not giving up.

"And why shouldn't someone else be able to do the same? You are in no condition to travel with your injured arm again.

"I tell you it is nothing and now when you heal me you will understand.

I am the one who has carried out the proceedings, who is in contact with the sheriff and who knows Swan and I can recognize him and discover him somewhere. On the other hand, if the opportunity presents itself to me, I must bill him for the cowardly ambush he has laid for me. For all these reasons, my duty compels me to return to Hutchinson and I will return.

As it was useless to insist, Margaret had to resign herself and took him to the cabin to seriously treat his arm, while the settlers took charge of the commissioner whom they invited to eat, since the man was hungry.

Margaret found that, indeed, Leslie's wound was more spectacular than serious, and after washing it well and applying a compress well soaked in arnica, she bandaged it with a piece of sheet.

"Are you convinced? He asked, holding her in his arms.

"Do not...! I think that I have been on the verge of losing you and that no one can know if what they have not achieved today they will achieve another day.

"This was a fortuitous accident, woman. Who would suspect that that buharro was here and that he was going to stumble upon him unexpectedly?

"But just as this one has arisen, another may arise and not come out as well as now.

"Things vary a lot now. Until yesterday, Swan could move freely, but after his task and knowing that he can be charged with attempted murder, he will be forced to hide and will not be able to walk freely. He himself has put dirt in his eyes by going so far in an effort to eliminate obstacles that prevent him from taking possession of our crops.

"Now we have to verify efforts to locate Adam, and even Swan, force them to speak out, confessing the first his crime and the second that he knew that what he was buying was the product of a robbery. Only in this way can we achieve that the original registration is annulled and placed in our name, freeing ourselves forever from new attempts at plunder.

"I also have to bring Bird with me when it is over and he is fit to travel. The poor man has more than paid for the naivety of informing his old companion of the reason that had led him to Hutchinson.

"I ask you to have serenity and accept things as they appear. If we had not made this trip, we would have found ourselves in a desperate situation, since it would not have been possible for me to bring this mess to light and one day we would have been stripped of what is so vital to us.

We have fought to secure these pieces of land, the mother earth that is our livelihood, and to continue to possess it by getting the right product out of it, we have to make all kinds of sacrifices. But the most serious ones, the ones that we have been able to overcome, offer us a more promising panorama and we should not stop halfway with exposing that they will strip us of everything.

"When this clears up and things are in their proper place, we will get married, we will dedicate all our efforts to consolidate what has been achieved and we will be as happy as we have dreamed of, because mother earth will continue to give us its fruits, who is grateful and knows how to give to her children, all the treasure that she hides in her entrails, when her children take care of her with the love that should be placed in a mother.

Margaret couldn't find the words to rebut her fiancé's. She was also a daughter of Mother Earth and she could not ignore that she had to defend her with all the tenacity of a true son.

"You're right, Leslie" ended up confessing. But, when I think that, for defending it, all it can give you as a reward is a hole covered in that land for which we fight so much, my flesh opens up.

"I realize it, but God is good and just and knows how to cover with his mantle those of us who honestly fight to live and want nothing more than what is ours.

"I am sure that this will end well and soon and that no new threats will arise. Let me finish the mission started and be calm, because I will know how to watch over my life, not only for me, but also for you, who for me is everything; you are the complement of that mother earth of our loves, because morally you are the best fruit that she has granted me.

The next day, Leslie and the commissioner spent it in the village preparing everything for the new trip. The colonists took care to prepare food for them for such a long journey and that rest suited them very well.

Leslie felt discomfort in his arm, but he tried to handle him and handle the revolver and found with satisfaction that he was not unable to handle a weapon.

Margaret took care to make him a packet of lint, bandages, and a bottle of arnica. The commissioner promised to cure him on the way, and when they reached Hutchinson if necessary, he would have the doctor see him.

After five boring and exhausting days on horseback, they finally arrived at the town one afternoon and without wasting time, they headed to the sheriff's offices.

The commissioner was in a hurry to inform his boss of what had happened, justifying the fact that he could not continue to be jealous of the dangerous trafficker.

When the sheriff saw them appear together in his office, he asked puzzled:

"Are you back here already, Mr. Simpson? And how does it come to my commissioner?

He stepped forward to say:

"Excuse me, boss, but something serious has forced me to let that toad of Swan escape from all surveillance. I had to do it if I wanted to save this man's life and I did not hesitate for a moment to fulfill that duty. If I have failed to do so, take whatever measures you think are the most just.

"I suppose that when he has done this, he must have had his reasons, Abel. Explain yourself and I will judge.

The commissioner explained how he had followed Swan and his laborers from afar on their visit to Abilene and how when the smuggler returned unsuccessful in his plan to surprise the settlers, he had arrived in time to prevent them by surprising Leslie on his trip from He returned to the village, they had surrounded him and were about to assassinate him if he did not intervene so in time.

"You will understand that my duty was to check if they had killed him, or if he was wounded and needed help. I chose to help him and had to let the gang get away.

"Well, Abel, I have nothing to reproach you for, for you have acted as your obligation was. That buharro can be located at some point, whereas a wounded man cannot be left bleeding on lost ground. I approve of his conduct and I have nothing to object to it.

"What I don't understand is how Swan has lost his sense of reality and has embarked on such a dangerous undertaking, which not only takes him many miles away from being able to enjoy ownership of those lands, but also places him out of the question. Law, charged with attempted murder.

"I believe that after the desperate effort he made to intimidate my colleagues and tear away their leases, he has understood that it is useless to fight to maintain that privilege so badly acquired and he is trying to get revenge on anyone.

"The fact that I have intervened so opportunely to undermine his projects has angered him against me, and when he recognized me among the rocks he wanted to eliminate me, possibly with the idea that I would not continue fighting to invalidate the registration. I can't find another explanation.

"Your thesis is very successful and if you have launched into that avenging career, be careful, do not surprise him again in worse conditions for you. What I do not understand is how he has not turned against Adam, who is the one who has put him in that well after all.

"Perhaps he does not know where he has gone and for that reason he is looking for other culprits for his failure.

"It is possible, but with what you have just committed, you will have to disappear from here and renounce to invoke any right that may benefit you, so that the validity of the registration is recognized. A favor to you because even in the desperate case that Adam was not found to justify the cancellation of the registration, neither Swan could legally settle on your land or transfer it to another, because the registry is ordered not to ratify new assignments.

"Yes, but this only solves things by half. We will not be under threat of eviction, but we will not be considered the legitimate owners of what is very much ours. The situation would be very ambiguous.

"I understand it, but at the moment there is nothing else. Let's hope that later on, you can get hold of Green, who is the key to all this.

"For now, I am going to send urgent notice to the Sheriff of Sterling, so that, if Swan is there, he can arrest him and send him well tied up, and if he is not, see to find out if he knows his whereabouts.

And for you I have good news. Bird is now out of danger, although he will still have to be in the hospital for ten or twelve days. He feels very animated and does nothing more than ask when they will let him out, to dedicate himself to looking for the rogue who was about to send him underground.

"I believe him capable of any madness in order to rehabilitate himself in our eyes, but we will not allow it. What you can't do, he can't do it, and if some help is needed, that's what I'm here for. I have warned that I will not return to Abilene until I have resolved this matter and now you will not feel uneasy about my delay.

"Good, Mr. Simpson. At the moment there is nothing to do as long as no clue is found. If you want, you can go to the hospital to visit your friend and reassure him.

"I'll do it right away. I'm very interested in Bird.

CHAPTER X

Devouring miles to leave behind the place where such unpleasant events had taken place, Swan arrived at Hutchinson together with his three pawns, since the fourth had been among the rocks dejected by Leslie's accurate shot, and gathering them, he gave them a hundred dollars to each other.

Take this for now; there may be more for you, but you have to earn it.

"We have had bad luck in that that guy who prevented us from ending that buharro appeared at such a critical moment, and since I suspect that it is some commissioner that the sheriff put in my footsteps to spy on me, I should not exhibit myself at the moment as long as I do not know in what situation have I placed myself.

"Adam is to blame for all this, he tricked me into scamming me ten thousand dollars. He assured me that the land was his and apparently he had stolen it from those settlers in a bad way.

"What Adam has been able to do in that sense does not matter to me, but it does matter to me that he has cheated me out of rejection, putting me in a situation that is becoming darker every day. I have tried to save that money and things have gone from bad to worse. I know that we will have to leave Kansas for a season, to move to some other state, but that does not matter. I will continue with the same business and you will continue to serve me as before, so you will lose nothing. After all, here we were becoming well known and elsewhere we can continue to operate with less risk.

"But I don't want to disappear without first paying off my debt to Adam. You know him well, you know the places he used to frequent when there was no work and it will be easier than for me to take steps to find out where he can walk at the moment.

"With ten thousand dollars in his pocket and with what he liked to play and hang out with girls from the gambling dens, he is sure to move somewhere where he can satisfy those whims.

"I would prefer that you discover him without him finding out, but if it is not possible and he asks you, you will tell him that I have not done anything yet with regard to the land, because I am in deals with several cattle points that interest me a lot and I cannot take care of of that now.

"As I am not going to Sterling in case they look for me there, I will seclude myself for a time at the home of a cousin of mine, who has some fields in Raymond. Whoever manages to find Adam's whereabouts will rush to that town to find out about the discovery. All you have to do is ask about the Kik fields and you will find me there.

"If you are willing to help me in that sense, I will thank you and I will keep it in mind, and if not, please say so so that I can take other steps that will lead to the result I want.

And with this promise from his pawns, Swan rushed to leave Hutchinson, fearing that the commissioner could return quickly and after reporting what happened to the sheriff, issue final orders to arrest him.

The fear was justified, since the stern sheriff had little knowledge of what happened on the banks of Smoky Hill, he had rushed to make urgent requests to search for Swan and not to neglect the essential capture of Adam.

The sheriff doubted that he could be easily located, since the crime of an attempted murder weighed on him, but Leslie was more optimistic, believing that he guessed that the miserable peon had been watching what happened to his victim and that, if he had read the news of his death without being able to open his mouth to testify, all danger to him was vanished with the death of the caravanner.

And Leslie was not mistaken, because Adam after learning that, despite the fury put into the coup, Bird had not died, the fear that he would testify accusing him had forced him to look for unlikely shelters, until, at last, a That day he had read the news of Bird's death in Hutchinson's journal, and this day he had taken a deep breath.

He had nothing to fear from the former caravanner or from the authorities; And as for Swan, he guessed that with no one to challenge the deal, he would find no obstacles to settling in Abilene either.

It was then that, leaving his intricate shelters, he decided to enjoy that wealth that he would never have dreamed of having in his pockets. He would live a princely life with him and, when it was over, he would start all over again.

And without much thought, he decided to move to Wichita.

This town was beginning to gain a reputation for being tough and attractive for those who had little to lose and a lot to gain.

The routes of the states that first timidly peered into Abilene in a great feat of mobility through the prairies had later been lengthened to Dodge City and, finally, seeking further business expansion, to Wichita.

And there the gambling dens, the houses with a low mark, the fetid and lethal environment that certain beings needed to breathe freely, had sprung up as if by charm and it was there that he could find the paradise of vice that he dreamed of.

And one fine day he entered the new livestock center following the footsteps of a bundle that served as a guide to locate the turbulent town.

Wichita was not a Hutchinson, as it was actually swelling in tune with the volume of the cattle and the equipment that came with it, but for a man like Adam who only sought pleasure and vice where it could be offered, Wichita enclosed all the charm he could wish for.

The gambling dens could not attract customers without something special to pull them, and thus, in all of them there was a cast of unfortunate girls, who had been plunged into the mud by their sad fate and rolled through it, they had reached that cattle-raising hell.

Adam found himself there at ease. The first thing he did was to equip himself as a powerful rancher in one of the town's warehouses and later, showing off what he looked like and was not, he dedicated himself to visiting the gambling dens in search of a girl who would fill his tastes, to make her part of his good luck.

Regardless of making love to a few, he did not stop visiting the gambling halls and during the first days of his stay in Wichita, fortune smiled at him in every way.

He had managed to interest one of the most sought-after girls among the many who alternated in those havens of vice, and, in addition, he had been lucky on the green carpet, obtaining profits that at some point came to double the money he had brought since Hutchinson.

This luck blinded him and he soon became one of the best known regulars at the gambling dens.

He spent without tax, he flattered the girls who were to his liking by giving them valuable gifts or money deliveries, trusting not in the one he had brought, but in the good luck that had touched him with its wings until then. It seemed as if in his blindness he believed that this manna would be eternal and would never be broken.

Until one good day "bad for Adam" one of the pawns highlighted by Swan made an appearance in Wichita to look for the clue of his old pawn.

Smarter than the other two, he thought that a man with a few thousand dollars and a passion for gambling and women could only find two cities to suit his tastes: Topeka or Wichita, which was beginning to be the empire. of vice. And he decided to go through the cattle town first. If he did not locate Adam there, he would continue to Topeka, sure to find him.

And he discovered it on the second day of being in the rough town.

He could not avoid giving hands to mouth with the persecuted laborer, since they met at the same door, when one was leaving a gambling den and the other entering. Adam, surprised, greeted his partner, saying:

"Devil, George ...! Like you around here?

The pawn quickly found a very plausible justification.

"I arrived yesterday driving a cattle drive.

"From Swan? Adam asked with some concern.

"Oh no...! Swan licensed us all as soon as you left. He had I don't know what kind of difficulties in the village and he told us that he planned to remain inactive for a few months. As we could not stand idly by, each of us looked for something to earn money. I was lucky; I found a friend who was looking for pawns to drive a bundle here and I hooked up with him.

"Bad trip, right?

Hell, but there was nothing else.

"And now what are you thinking to do?

"Go back with the team to Hutchinson; we're leaving tomorrow

"I realize, there is no where to work here, if not in that.

"Good; and what do you do?

"You see, giving me a good life.

"I can see that. You dress like a potentate.

"I have been lucky playing.

"Apparently, you were born with a lucky star.

"I can not complain.

"Do you plan to be here a long time?

"At least while luck smiles on me and money lasts. Here you will find what is not found in many places.

"I envy you, boy, but I, who have bad luck playing, cannot aspire to give myself a life like you. I will reserve my pay until I find something more productive.

"Well, that won't stop you from agreeing to have dinner with me and hang out at a joint tonight. Don't worry about my expense.

"That being the case, I accept.

Adam allowed his former partner to dance with the artist, not without warning her that if she asked him questions about his life and position, he would claim that he owned a huge ranch that he had inherited from an uncle of hers in eastern Kansas.

The laborer took as many notes as he could about Adam's customs in the village and, at dawn, said goodbye to him, claiming that he had no choice but to leave. Adam magnanimously took out a handful of bills and offered them to her, saying:

"Here, in case you find yourself out of work for some time. Take them without scruples, it has cost me very little work to win them.

The pawn accepted them. Later he found out that he had given her seventy dollars.

As quickly as possible, he returned to Hutchinson, and from there he made his way to the rendezvous with Swan. He was looking forward to the two hundred dollars the dealer had offered.

When Swan saw him appear in his kinsman's fields, his eyes sparkled with joy.

Good news, George?

"Enough for you to give me the promised money. I know where Adam is and I've talked to him.

"Bad done, I told you that ...

"I could not avoid it. We faced each other as he entered a Wichita joint and I left.

"So he's in Wichita?

"Yes, he dresses like a potentate, alternates in the best venues, plays hard and has won the affection of one of the most attractive beauties in the town.

"You have a good time, don't you?

"He says that he has made a lot of money at the gaming tables and, because of the way of life he leads, that is the way it should be. He plans to be there indefinitely, he stays at the "Hotel Kansas" and alternates with preference in "The Silver Dollar".

"Didn't he ask you any questions about me or was he surprised to see you there?

"I told him that you had licensed us all, because I was planning to remain inactive for a season and that I had joined a team of cattle drivers. I made him believe that I had arrived the previous afternoon and that I was leaving the next day. This is all.

"Good, George. Here's the two hundred dollars and be on the lookout for if I need you at some point. When I settle my business with Adam, we'll start over, even if it's in other places. I cannot remain inactive for long.

The peon said goodbye to him to return to Hutchinson and Swan, overcome by a dull anger that did not allow him to control his nerves, prepared to march to Wichita in search of his former pawn.

And since George had given him all the details he needed to locate Adam, he set out to hunt him down when he could least suspect it.

He stationed himself near the hotel where the false potentate was staying and waited patiently for it to fall at night. If Adam frequented the gambling dens until dawn, he hoped to see him leave the hotel at any moment.

And he did not see his hopes frustrated, because at about half past ten, the ex-laborer, made an arm of the sea, left the hotel smoking a magnificent Virginia cigar to go to the "Silver Dollar."

Swan followed him at a distance. This was not the most appropriate time to approach him, due to the many people who passed through the streets; he would have to arm himself with patience and wait for the night to pass and, at dawn, when he left the gambling den, go out to meet him and settle the accounts that were pending.

For the trafficker it was an agonizing wait that ended up unhinging his nerves. His patience was wearing thin, despite his efforts, and in more than a moment he was tempted to enter the joint with revolver in hand and shoot him.

But he was able to hold out despite everything and when dawn was approaching and the place had already been completely empty, he saw him emerge at the door, in the light of the lamp that hung from the upper doorway.

But with infinite rage he observed that he did not go out alone. He was accompanied by a tall, blond girl, wrapped in a wide shawl to protect herself from the cool early morning air.

Adam gallantly offered his arm to accompany her and Swan, unable to resist any longer, leapt out of the shadows and in several strides stood in front of the couple, bellowing:

"Adam, son of a wolf ...! You're going to. pay for the work you have done to me!

Adam, realizing the danger, let go of the girl's arm and put his hand to the side, but late, because the dealer's revolver thundered twice and the former laborer dropping his weapon, put his hands to his chest and fell collapsed. on the ground, while his companion, terrified, screamed hysterically for help.

Swan caught distant footsteps approaching and, running, he lost himself down a dark alley, fleeing before they could stop him.

He believed that he had killed Adam and this was enough for him, but he was not willing to let himself be caught.

And as he had left everything ready for flight, he ran through various deserted alleys until he reached the place where he had left his horse, ready to set out.

He had acted in a place too far away, where he was not known to anyone and if Adam had died as he supposed, find out who had killed him.

It would be one more incident of the many that occurred due to rivalries in dirty matters, and once the body was buried, the file would be closed with the helpful phrase of "killed by an unknown hand."

When again he found himself under the protection of his cousin's property, he justified his absence by saying that he had gone to resolve a cattle matter and that for the moment he planned to spend a season of rest. He would stay with his cousin for a week or two, and then he would take a trip to New Mexico to pulse the atmosphere in case it suited him to stay there.

However, he was tormented by a doubt as before it had tormented Adam, and it was the uncertainty of not knowing fixedly if his former pawn had died or not.

But this was not going to be easy for him to check. Wichita was too far away and the news couldn't get to him. He would have to settle for wishing the shots had been effective.

But if Adam saved himself and reported him, he didn't expect anyone to bother with too many inquiries to find him. The life of a guy like Adam was worthless especially in latitudes like those and no one was going to bother to mobilize the entire state to look for him. It is true that he could say that he lived in Sterling, but since he was not going to return to that town, let them look for him as much as they wanted.

The days had passed without variation at Hutchinson. Leslie was spending what little money she had been able to set aside in anticipation of dire needs and did not solve anything that would clarify the situation.

No one gave a reason for Adam and nothing had been heard from Swan again. It seemed as if the earth had swallowed them up, and yet they had to be somewhere not far away, and fate made it impossible to find them.

Bird was recovering quickly. His extremely serious wound had healed and he was impatient to be discharged to feverishly indulge in the search for his traitorous former caravan companion.

Until one day, the sheriff managed to hook the thread of the track that would lead him to Adam and Swan, through the conduit he could least suspect.

It was on the occasion of the arrest of George, Swan's pawn who had just arrived from Wichita. George, after receiving the two hundred dollars from the dealer, had gone into a gambling den, got drunk, had a major fight with a rancher who he hit with a bottle and one of the sheriff's commissioners stopped him and took him to the Offices.

And it was there that the other commissioner, the one who had followed Swan and his team to the vicinity of Abilene, recognized him instantly.

When he gave the sheriff of such recognition, the man with the star subjected the laborer to a rude and exhausting interrogation, to the point of forcing him to spout everything he knew.

And what he knew the sheriff was unaware of was his quest to locate Adam, his encounter with him, his return to report to Swan, and the gratification Swan had given him for the news.

The sheriff rushed to find the smuggler, but he had already left for Wichita. His cousin didn't know where he had gone, but Swan had told him that he would be back after a week.

At the moment there was nothing I could do, if it wasn't wait; but he put a discreet guard around the fields of Swan's cousin, to stop Swan as soon as he returned. And immediately sent a long telegram to the sheriff of Wichita, interested in the capture of Adam and, if possible, that of Swan, since he assumed with good reason that the trafficker had gone to the cattle town only with the obsession of making anyone disappear thus he had deceived him. Perhaps he was still believed that, by shutting up Adam's tongue forever, it would not be possible to clarify the first registration and could at some point ascertain the legality of his purchase.

Twenty-four hours later, the sheriff received the reply from Wichita. The town sheriff would telegraph him saying:

> I received your telegram and when I was about to verify records, events have rushed.
>
> This morning, when leaving a joint accompanied by an artist, the one called Adam Greene received two bullets in the chest, which if they are not fatal could be. As he was able to testify, the aggressor is a trafficker from those surroundings, named Swan. He lives in a town called Sterling.
>
> Following his instructions, I have kept Adam in one of my cages, where the doctor comes to treat him. This ensures that within eight or ten days you will be able to travel, if necessary, although with certain precautions.
>
> I await further news from you to proceed.

Leslie's joy was enormous when the sheriff realized how much he knew. Adam was in the net without being able to escape and as for Swan, it would be a matter of days to get hold of him.

"What do you intend to do? Leslie asked.

"This is what I am wondering. I don't trust myself leaving Adam in the hands of my partner so that he can refer me to someone there. There could be a bribe or something similar, if as he says, Adam handles a lot of money and would prefer to send for him.

"But I have only two commissioners. One is on the lookout for Swan in case he returns, and the other is not enough for such a long drive. I need more people.

"That can be fixed. I can accompany your commissioner and, between the two of us, take care of Adam and bring him here. As you will suppose, you will not be able to bribe me for much money you have.

"I already suppose and since you offer to help my commissioner, I accept the offer. From what my partner says, it will take about eight days to be fit to travel. If a cart is rented to bring it, the trip will consume you almost that time and you will arrive just to take care of the ruffian. In the meantime, I will try to capture Swan, and if I succeed, the matter will be resolved in no time.

"For my part, I am ready to leave when you say.

"They can do it in the morning. My commissioner will take care of arranging everything for the trip.

"Very good. I just want to ask you to be on the lookout for when Bird is discharged. Take care of him, don't let him leave here and assure him that everything will be fixed in a few days.

"Don't worry, I'll do it that way.

The next day, the sheriff and Leslie left for Wichita with an arrest warrant signed by the sheriff and a letter to the sheriff. The matter was in the process of being solved and Leslie was jumping for joy.

On the third day after the two of them had left in search of Adam, Swan returned to his cousin's fields. He was far from suspecting that this time things were going to get worse than ever and that he had stumbled that could no longer be fixed.

The commissioner let him arrive and when he least expected it, he made his appearance at the cabin, surprising the dealer and his cousin.

The commissioner, who was the same one who had saved Leslie's life among the rocks, intimidated him by saying:

"Mr. Swan, you are being detained by order of the Hutchinson sheriff.

"Me? For what reason?

"He is accused of having tried to murder an Abilene settler.

"Me? Who can prove that absurdity?

"I, who was the one who intervened when you and three pawns under your command tried to shoot him down. It is useless to deny it, because, in addition, one of the peons is detained, who has confessed everything.

The smuggler's teeth gritted fiercely.

"This is a trap and I will not fall for it.

"That tells the sheriff. Raise your arms for me to strip you of the revolver and then follow me.

Swan hesitated for a moment, but obeyed and when the commissioner grasped the butt of the weapon, Swan tried to drive his knee into his chest, but the commissioner, who was not a rookie, arched his body in time and the blow was unsuccessful. Not so his, because of an applied impressive head butt, deprived him of knowledge.

And carrying the body of the trafficker on his shoulder, he left the cabin and placing his load on the back of the horse, he prepared to return to the town.

By the time he got to it, Swan had regained consciousness, but well handcuffed, he was powerless to turn against the commissioner again.

The sheriff took care of him and forcing him to sit in front of him, he said:

"Mr. Swan, when people greedily maneuver and claim to own what is worth a hundred for five, they generally end up losing everything and with it, freedom and who knows what else.

"You. He believed he was doing a great business buying Adam for a piece of shit that was worth a lot of money and when he realized that his greed had led him to make a bad deal, he did not resign himself to losing, but turned against everyone and spite him. It has led you to commit a series of actions that will cost you dearly, since you are accused with evidence of two assassination attempts. One, in the person of a settler from Abilene. and another in the person of Adam, whom you have expressly sought in Wichita to send him to Hell.

"If what you wanted was to close your mouth so that you could not declare how you did with the two documents that served to verify the first record, you have failed, because Adam has not died, but, even if he had died, you .I would never have been able to claim those lands because it was out of the law to conserve them.

Swan stirred angrily.

"I did not know how they had come into his hands, because if I knew that he had committed a crime, he would not have bought them.

"Anyway, it will be a comfort to you to know that Adam will not be better off. Also weighing on him is an accusation of attempted murder with robbery and the jurors will not be shy when judging him. I'm afraid you two are going to dance together in the same tree.

"I will be consoled if I see him dance before I do.

"That, luck will decide. And now, if you have nothing to argue in your favor, you can only wait for the ruling when the cause is seen.

"When that time comes, I will try to defend myself.

The sheriff locked him up again and prepared to await the return of Leslie and his sheriff.

They arrived a few days later, taking the one who caused so much distress in the cart, tightly tied.

Dan had lost all his arrogance and cynicism. He realized the trap he was in and the panic of suffering the consequences had sunk him morally and materially.

The sheriff treated him harshly and subjected him to a brutal interrogation, but Adam, believing that Bird had died as he read in the newspaper, insisted on not confessing his crime.

"I didn't kill anyone" he roared. I found those papers in an envelope in the middle of the street and realizing that they had a good value if I hurried to register those lands in my name, I did. They may accuse me of misappropriation, but not of any crime.

"Do you think you can't be accused of that?

"I challenge you to present evidence. Let's see who saw me kill or try to kill anyone and bring me the victim.

"Didn't you read that your victim had died? Who do you think was the man they found dying in the alley of Los Sauces? Is he going to deny that he knew Victor Bird?

"I don't know who that Bird is, I've never heard of him. If he should have had the papers and lost them, that does not mean that I was the author of his death. I found the papers on the street. Perhaps the one who killed him when he fled lost them.

"Is that your last word?

"I have no other and I repeat that I challenge you to prove that I killed that man.

"Well, we'll see if it gets done.

And the next day, when Bird had just left the hospital with the discharge in his pocket, Leslie took him to the sheriff's offices. This, in revenge to the war that that matter had given him, had prepared a surprise show for Adam. The surprise of facing him with Bird, whom the ruffian believed was already rotting his bones underground.

Taking him out of the cage and pushing him towards the office, he said sarcastically:

"Adam, he introduced you to who can attest that you tried to assassinate him in the alley of Los Sauces.

The ruffian was left as pale as wax when confronted with the former caravanner, and for a moment it seemed that he was going to collapse from the fierce shock, but reacting brutally, with an unexpected leap he launched himself at Bird, bellowing:

"You, damn your stamp!

Handling and everything, it seemed that he was going to fall on the convalescent ex-caravan, crushing him with the weight of his body before the sheriff and Leslie reacted and could catch him, but it was not necessary, because Bird in the height of his anger, activated the leg as the ruffian leaped on him and applied the sole of his hard boot to his face with such force that he threw him backward against the front door.

Adam fell to the ground, bleeding dramatically from his mouth and nose, and it was Bird who had to be held, as he tried to throw himself on his enemy to destroy him with his claws.

Dragging Adam's battered body, they carried him back to the cage, while Leslie tried to calm her partner. The test had been too harsh for both of them, each in one sense, but enough not to need another confrontation.

The matter was clear enough in every way. Adam had confessed to having searched the land improperly, even though he denied the robbery and attempted murder. Now, exposed, he could no longer deny and the judges when the case was heard, would annul the registration for both Adam and Swan, awarding it to their true owners.

Leslie's tenacity had finally achieved what was fair.

CHAPTER XI

MOTHER EARTH

Two days later, after verifying the corresponding report against Adam and Swan and presenting the case to the competent authorities so that they could signal the hearing of the case, Leslie and Bird decided to return to the town.

They could no longer delay the return. In Abilene they would be haunted by their fate, since they had been away from their homes for too many days and since the trial would still take at least three or four weeks, the return was imposed.

But the sheriff reassured them about the future. The matter was so clear that when a sentence was passed against the two ruffians, another would be handed down, annulling the registration and ordering that it be awarded to its true owners.

However, Leslie promised to return after a month.

In the meantime, he would take care of their interests and at the same time bring joy and tranquility to a hundred homes where at that time restlessness reigned.

During the trip, Bird stated contritely:

"I am ashamed to introduce myself to our colleagues. I have been stupid and trusting, and because of me they have all been exposed to losing their properties. I doubt they will forgive me.

"Don't be picky," Leslie replied. They know that you are a decent man and that it was all a chance. I can assure you that they have been as anxious for your life as for your properties.

"God pay you all, Leslie, and you in particular, who have risked your life to put together what I so stupidly screwed up.

"You can't be too good, because how you get so stupid that you think others are as good as you.

"You are right, Leslie. We men do not know how to be grateful enough for what the earth gives us. We would like the fruit, but avoiding sweating on the ground to obtain it. If we did not exist the whole host of tough men, willing to suffer the inclemencies of the weather scratching the bark, then we would see if others would know how to value our effort.

With these bitter disquisitions, the couple reached the vicinity of the town. Never before had they felt such emotion, perhaps because until then they had felt like men who lived on loan and now they knew themselves as absolute owners of everything that made up their lives and homes.

The more advanced settlers, when they saw the wagon that was rolling slowly, began to spread the word of the arrival of the two men, and soon the work was abandoned and everyone flocked to meet them with the eagerness reflected on their faces.

They had been in the most complete ignorance of all the vicissitudes suffered by the two colonists in Hutchinson and they were overwhelmed by the doubt of what could have happened with the dominion of their lands.

Everyone surrounded the two heroes of the adventure, harassing them with questions and Leslie to calm them, shouted:

"One moment, companions. You will know everything in due time and in order, but to calm your concerns I will anticipate that this matter has been resolved. The two most fearsome enemies that had come our way, are imprisoned and accused of robbery and murder. They will be judged and sentenced shortly, and when this happens the judges will decree the invalidity of that record and will order that it be placed in our names.

"So everyone calm down and don't harass us more than necessary. We have spent exhausting days carrying out intense procedures, I have had to make a very heavy trip to Wichita, to take care of the ruffian who injured Bird and stole our documents and now we have also had a hard day until here. Let us regain strength and then you will know everything with the greatest amount of data.

A hooray! clamorously welcomed Leslie's words. Many embraced him excitedly, others jumped for joy and some took Bird in their arms and carried him towards the fields, carrying him on their shoulders with the natural emotion of the old caravanner.

As the large crowd of settlers surrounding the wagon cleared, Leslie was able to get off it. A short distance away, with tears of joy in her eyes, Margaret waited for the moment to be able to approach her fiancé, and he, advancing towards her, opened his arms to receive her, shouting:

"Margaret ...!

For a few minutes they were tense, holding each other feverishly. Neither of them could speak, and it was Leslie who first regained her composure, saying:

"Well, Margaret, I suppose your nerves will have settled by now and all your worries will have died.

"Yes, dear, now yes, but until now ... how many nights of anguish, fear, uncertainty I have spent, thinking about what could have happened to you! It has been almost three weeks of absence that I do not wish them on my worst enemy.

A little later, the settler gave a faithful account of everything that had happened and explained how by pure chance, when one of Swan's pawns was arrested, his whereabouts and his feat of moving to Wichita to shoot down Swan had been discovered. his old pawn.

Margaret had listened longingly to him, and when she finished her story, she commented:

"Do you think that ... they will really annul that registration and put it in our name?

"I have no doubt, my dear. The sheriff assured me formally and it stands to reason. With Adam having to acknowledge that he tried to kill Bird only to seize the papers and register the land in his name, it is a demonstration that he belongs to us and the judges will pass the appropriate sentence.

"On the other hand, I have put on record that Adam stole more than eight hundred dollars from Bird that he had in his pocket to make some purchases and since they have found Adam in his pocket almost seven thousand, they will return them to us and perhaps more as compensation to the damages suffered.

"Everything, as you can see, has been solved, and there is no fear that the matter will recur and now that I have fully informed you of everything, allow me to take a look at my lands. I have been away from here for almost a month and a half without taking care of my interests and this does worry me now.

"Well follow me and stop worrying. You will see that your crops are as in order as those of the others. We have all contributed our efforts to take care of them as our own and you will not have to blame anyone for abandonment that has not existed. Come.

He took her by the arm and they walked over to where Leslie kept his plot.

Next to it was a mound and, gaining its small top, they gazed around them.

It was mid-afternoon, the sun of the already coming summer, shining with force, splendor, and where the landscape was covered, only waves of blondes and overgrown ears could be seen that, already in season, only awaited the cutting edge of the sickle to be reaped the harvest.

Leslie with tears in her eyes and dominated by an intense emotion, took his fiancee by the waist and commented:

"Isn't this beautiful that we behold, Margaret?

"Of course it is, dear.

"Yes, it is beautiful and exciting. Perhaps for many, the contemplation of what surrounds us does not have a great meaning. Many will look at it with indifferent eyes, as something natural and often seen, but not us. We have to admire it with different eyes because it is our work, the product of effort, something that carries in its entrails much of our sap spilled in a muscular effort on mother earth, to make it bear fruit for the good of all.

"I was born a colonist because God wanted it that way and I have never complained about this hard and exhausting inclination. Everything that is created has its beauty and this also has it, although many do not know how to understand it.

For this reason, many times, when in populated cities where the heartbeat of the earth is not pulsed because it is far from it, I have seen how people have felt pleasant with an engineer, an architect or any other man of science and us He has treated us with indifference, saying at the most, Bah, a peasant! I have felt hurt and indignant.

"Nobody has stopped to think how important is the one that draws a bridge or erects a great building, as the one that plucks its fruits from the ground after much sweat and anguish. We are all creditors of something and deserve the same treatment and respect.

"Only when the great catastrophes have devastated the lands, brought down the crops and reduced the articles that we offer them with our sweat, have they been moved, but not by us, who saw ourselves in ruin, but because for the others have been in short supply of wheat or flour. Only then have they realized a little of what Mother Earth means to humanity, even if they ignored what these tremendous catastrophes could have meant for us.

"But it doesn't matter, Margaret; we live in our little world and we are happy in it. For us, mother earth is everything. We know how to value what we ask of her and what she gives us, and if she gives us enough to live on, we are grateful to her and pamper her for what she is: our material mother.

"Do you see that huge harvest that this year gives us in return for our effort? For she is our happiness, our home, God's blessing for our love and our tranquility. I know that in these days the railroad is going to start operating and that this will allow us to dispose of all the stored grain and the one that we are going to collect. We will sell it, we will have money to complete what we lack and the town will grow, prosper and have things that are very necessary and that we will make sure that they are not lacking.

"There will be a church, a school for the boys, a small casino for our modest and familiar parties; and one day, this people born out of nowhere, because a handful of tough men of good will wanted it that way, will become part of the nation's geography and will be marked on maps as something tangible. That day, we will all feel proud of it, because each and every one of us put our grain of wheat "never better applied the phrase" so that the wish would become a reality.

"And we owe everything to the mother earth, which was waiting for us here eager to receive the caress of our rough hands, to offer us the fruit that it kept in its entrails and that no one had come to collect.

"Yes, Leslie, we will owe it to her and to our efforts.

"Fair, but the effort must be applied where it pays off. Sowing in the sand is not profitable, it must be done here, where Mother Earth can compensate for that effort.

"And now, I will tell you something that will make you very happy. I have promised to return to Hutchinson in a month, which will be the date on which the trial will be seen and everything will be solved. To verify this, to be sure that the registration has been legalized in our name, I will return, but delaying the trip a bit. First we will reap the harvest and then ... I will load the wagon of wheat and you and your father will come with me.

"We will sell the wheat there, with what they give us we will buy what we need to dress as God intended and get married right there, without having to wait for the church to rise here and whoever can come. We will return married and nothing will disturb the happiness that we have earned with so much sweat. Seem to you?

She jumped on his neck, stamping a passionate kiss on his mouth as she affirmed:

"That is how I want it, because that is how you want it. Blessed are you, Leslie!

"And blessed be the land that has given us the possibility of being as happy as we have dreamed of.

And there, at the top of the small top of the mound, both tightly embraced, they smiled happily, while the wind rocked the tapestry of spikes that seemed to greet them as they bent over the earth and the river glided murmuring who knew what phrases of love and happiness for the passionate bride and groom.

END